AGENTS of the ANCIENTS

EPISODE 1

THE GRISTMILL ARTIFACT

SHANE GREGORY

Churnbug Studio
ISBN: 978-0692438749

CHURNBUG

CHAPTER 1

When I first met Thaddeus Soosen, he was a mere apparition, see-through and chest-deep in the concrete floor of my dad's museum. He appeared there on the afternoon of June 5 without warning, and he was just as surprised and confused by it as I.

My dad, Peter Bright, Ph.D., did not actually own the Old Mill Museum in Kinsville, but he had been the director of the nonprofit for eight years. In all that time, he had never mentioned anything odd happening. He let me work there after school and during the summer for two of those years. Even though there were a few interesting items on display, most of my time there was boring and uneventful.

The museum has occupied an old, repurposed gristmill for almost four decades, and to my knowledge, its previous directors had never warned my dad there was anything amiss with the building's history that would lead one to suspect ghosts (not that I believed in such a thing). Sure, there was the occasional out-of-the-ordinary or eccentric visitor, but that is to be expected when dealing with the public.

On that afternoon in June, the museum was just scraping by. Even though out-of-town visitors enjoyed stopping in, my dad never had been able to get the locals very interested in the place. There were more exciting things to hold their attention, I suppose. Private grants and government funding were cut a little more each year. Dad tried everything in his modest bag of tricks to get people to donate. He would never let on, but he was stressed.

I told him we needed something to draw the crowds, like Sasquatch fur or a giant ball of rubber bands. It didn't have to be anything historical or even genuine, just something to get people in the door. He wouldn't go for it. He told me, "I am not P. T. Barnum. We won't compromise our legitimacy by using gimmicks. We are above that."

However, he wasn't above begging. Dad spent the last week of my junior year in high school compiling a list of wealthy philanthropists and foundations known to be generous to historical museums. When summer vacation was finally underway, he packed his bags and left me alone to hold the fort the first two weeks of June while he traveled around country to plead his case to the potential donors.

One time, a little girl on a field trip to the museum asked how old the building was. When I told her it was more than one hundred fifty years, she said, "Buildings that old always have at least one ghost." She was just a mouthy kid, but she said it with such certainty that I didn't dare laugh. Her declaration about old buildings and ghosts clicked the moment I locked eyes with Thaddeus Soosen, and once my initial shock settled, I believed dad's begging days were over. I had found us a money-maker—a bona fide haunting.

Or so I thought.

June 5 was the day that tornado plowed into the north side of Kinsville. I had kept an eye on the weather all that day, and I knew the storm front was moving in. I liked thunderstorms, so the approaching dark clouds and rumbles were sort of comforting. Most of the time, the severe weather alerts didn't bother me too much. The local meteorologists tend to err on the side of caution and act like the sky is falling every time there's a little thunder. The weather radio is always going off for something, especially in the spring. I try not to get too concerned until the city activates the warning siren. When that happens, I know it is serious. That day, it was serious.

The tornado siren, which was a block away at the fire station, wailed so loudly I found it difficult to form a complete thought. It scared me, but I kept my head enough to move into what I thought would be the safest place in the building—an interior meeting room. Once there, I crawled under the heavy table and waited for the all clear.

The wind picked up outside, and rain beat hard against the windows of the museum. The large, metal casement windows were the kind you often find in old factories from the late 19th and early 20th centuries. Some of the panes had been replaced over the years, but the actual windows were original to the building. Even though they had survived for more than one hundred fifty years, I was concerned about the pressure from this particular storm.

The roar from outside grew louder. Lightning flashed. I whispered assurances to myself. The power went out. Then it was like time slowed. Lightning reflected on the tall, brick walls. It was less like lightning and more like the way a television will light up a dark room changing with the scenes on the screen. When it didn't stop, I was intrigued. I took a chance and pulled myself from under the table.

The huge metal framework of the windows set in the front of the building glowed blue. Tendrils of light licked out as if searching. Individual panes of glass cracked then shattered. Meanwhile, outside, it turned as dark as dusk.

One of those crooked fingers of blue electricity arced out and touched the wall to the right of the window. Another leapt out to the concrete floor. It danced there a moment, then slowly traced around the exhibits. It was as if it had intelligence. Twice it halted and crawled up a pedestal like it was feeling its way around. Entranced, I shut out everything else—the scream of the siren, the roar of the wind, the breaking panes.

Then the finger of blue light stopped near a particular glass case that contained artifacts from the era of the American Civil War. The metal items in the case took on the same blue glow. Then, suddenly, everything was dark again. I blinked to get my eyes to adjust, and there he was.

He materialized in the dim light near a Civil War display. It wasn't the full form of a man, but rather from the chest up as if the museum floor was a smooth pond into which he had waded. And he wasn't solid; I could see right through him. I got to my feet and took a step closer.

He turned in place, peering around. He had long hair tucked under a bowler hat, handlebar mustache and goatee, and he wore a tweed frockcoat.

He noticed me, and his eyes widened.

"Madness!" he exclaimed.

Even though he was no more than ten feet from me, his voice sounded far away. Then he noticed he was immersed in the floor. With some effort, he pulled his right arm up and out and felt the surface of the painted, gray concrete. I had presumed his transparence meant he was a ghost or some sort of spiritual projection and as such could pass through solid matter with ease; however, the floor was affecting his movements. His eyes found mine again. He reached out to me. He was scared.

"By God, man, help me!" his muffled voice cried.

At that moment, a limb from the redbud tree outside stabbed through the front window, and the noise of the world flooded into my awareness again. We were both startled. Leaves and small bits of debris flew in through the broken windows. He pushed toward me and stretched out his hand for mine like a man stuck in quicksand.

"Train's a comin'!" he yelled.

I heard it too. It was the sound of a freight train.

4

CHAPTER 2

The churning roar of the approaching twister grew louder, and my ears popped from the pressure. I was certain I'd be sucked out. Then, from the floor of the museum, an orb of blue light arose straight up between me and the transparent man. The grapefruit-sized ball of energy climbed into the air. It was about to bump into the ceiling when it stopped, expanded, and blew outward without a sound. The entire room was filled with bright, blue light.

And then it was over. Outside, the storm was gone, and the sun shone again. I shook my head and blinked down at the man poking out of the floor.

"What just happened?" I asked him.

"Are the demons about?" was his shouted reply as he struggled to climb out of the floor. "Are they loose?"

"This isn't Hell," I said in a whisper more to myself than to him.

The tornado siren silenced, but the sirens of emergency vehicles still screamed nearby.

The man reached out to me again. "Sir, I feel myself j'inin' with this stone. I swear I'll be swallowed up if you withhold your help a moment longer."

Reluctantly and with some fear, I stepped forward and extended my hand. He stretched and strained then gripped my hand. It wasn't like real flesh. It was more like vibrating dough. My fingers sank into him or maybe he sank into me; either way, we were merging. Alarmed by this, I attempted to pull away, but he grabbed my forearm near the elbow with his other hand.

"Not until I'm free," he said through clenched teeth.

His less-than-solid hands oozed into my skin and touched my bones. A fine vibration settled in. It wasn't painful, but it was uncomfortable and unnerving. I again tried to pull myself free. By this time, he had managed to get a leg out, but it was as if the concrete was fresh and not yet set. He sank again.

"You must do the work!" he yelled. "There's no purchase for my boots! Put your back into it."

I relented and took his arm with my other hand and leaned back. He didn't weigh very much, which I attributed to his lack of solidity. There was some resistance, and his fingers moved down the inside of my arm, but once I put forth the effort, I was able to pull him out. I dragged him a few feet on his belly then jerked myself free. He started to sink again and rolled out to the surface onto his back. Again, the floor crept up over the sides of his arms. He pushed up to his knees. This made him sink faster.

"Spread yourself out flat," I said.

He rolled out again onto his back with his arms spread wide as if he was about to make a snow angel. His coat fell open, and I spied a gold watch chain coming out of a pocket of his paisley vest. Inside that pocket, whatever was on the other end of that watch chain emitted a blue glow through the fabric of the vest. There was a revolver tucked into a holster under his arm.

Slowly, his body eased into the floor.

"Damnation!" he shouted and rolled again back on top.

"I don't know how to help you!" I cried in frustration. Then I remembered I was talking to a ghost.

There were voices coming from the street as people started to venture out and inspect the damage from the storm.

The man noticed something on the wall behind me, and his eyes narrowed. "They are here," he growled. He struggled to get erect, reached into his coat, and came out with the revolver just as the floor enveloped his feet. I didn't know if a ghost's gun could harm me, but I didn't take any chances. I dropped to the floor and covered my head. He fired at something behind me near the ceiling. The report of the weapon was loud, but, like the man's voice, it had a faraway sound to it.

"I believe it's just the one!" he called out as he tried to run. He stepped high through the exhibition space so he could pull his foot out of the floor with each stride. It reminded me of someone running in knee-deep water or snow. His attention was on something in the other gallery. He passed into the next room, and his gun went off again. "I'm missin' my astra. Is it here?"

I stared at the spot where he had last been and I tried to make sense of the past few minutes. Tornado, blue lights, a ghost that keeps sinking into the floor, functioning ghost gun....

"Astra!" he yelled. "Where is it?!"

Is he talking to me?

I stood, took a few timid steps, and peeked into the next room. The ghost had his back to me. He stared up to the far left corner of the ceiling and pointed his weapon that direction. I followed his line of sight and gasped.

There was a naked man up there—that's what I thought at first. It was shaped like a man, and it had the same features, but there were small differences that let me know something was not right about it. Its skin was pale and slightly yellow. The hairless body was thin, but not frail; the muscles were clearly defined. Its eyes were totally black. Its nose, chin, and cheekbones were somewhat oversized and sharp. Its ears were undersized. If I'd seen it dressed in jeans and a t-shirt and walking down the street, I might have done a double-take, but

7

it could pass as an odd-looking human so long as it wasn't scrutinized. But hanging from the ceiling and completely naked, it didn't look human at all.

The ghost was pointing a gun at it, so I presumed the thing was not only not human, but also not good. The gun went off again and, ghost gun or not, the bullet entered one of the exposed rafters, splintering the wood. The naked, yellow creature on the ceiling scurried, upside down, from one rafter to the next. It moved over the ghostly man, headed in my direction like a spider. When it was directly over me, it tilted its head back to look down on me. I noticed then how large its mouth was, the slit extending well back into the jaw.

Its plump lips parted to reveal a row of teeth like a saw blade. The revolver went off one last time. The creature tensed then dropped more than fifteen feet from the ceiling and landed in front of me with an audible smack. Thick, black blood ejaculated from a hole in its head. Then the thing slowly sank into the concrete floor until it was completely buried.

The man in old-timey clothes was already wading his way over to me. I'd read ghost stories, but all of this was new to me.

"I think it's just the one," he repeated.

At that moment, a police radio squawked outside the broken front window followed by the low voice of a man. They were either coming to check on my safety after the storm or they were investigating the gunfire. The ghost man stopped and turned, trying to find the source of the noise and voices.

"Police," I said as an explanation. "Hide!"

He immediately ran in the opposite direction. There was nowhere for him to hide that way except to exit through the back door.

The front door of the museum swung open, and a city police officer stepped inside with the heel of his hand on the butt of his holstered sidearm. He mumbled something into the mike attached to his shoulder then regarded me with suspicion and concern.

"You okay, son?" he said.

I glanced into the other room where the ghost man was making a retreat. He had reached the back wall. He looked over his shoulder at me then walked right through the wall and disappeared outside.

"Are you okay?" said the cop.

I continued to stare at the wall in the other room.

"Hey!"

"Yes," I said, startled. "Yeah, I'm sorry. I'm just...there's some damage to the building."

"Are you injured? Do you need medical assistance?"

"No," I replied.

"What was that noise I heard?" he said, unconvinced. "It sounded like gunfire."

"Oh," I said, stalling. I stared at my shoes the way I do when I'm trying to come up with a lie. "I don't know maybe...." There was a glob of the yellow creature's black blood on my shoe. I let out a whimper.

"Maybe what?" he said.

"I don't know," I said. "I think the electrical box...the breaker box...I think it was popping or something."

"Turn off the main breaker," he said. "Call someone in to check it out. We're closing this end of town to incoming traffic so they can clear away some of the debris. If you can get home, do so."

I stared at that black spot. It was really there.

"Are you sure you're okay?" he said.

I nodded. "Yes, sir. Sorry. Thanks for checking on me."

He returned the nod and left.

I waited a moment to make sure the officer wouldn't come back then I ran through the exhibits in the gallery to the rear exit. I paused a moment beneath the very real bullet hole in the ceiling then opened the back door. Trash, sticks, and leaves were scattered on the back sidewalk. A little farther out in the back lot was a piece of white vinyl siding and some shingles.

Some of the neighboring business owners were out surveying the storm damage. A block away, firemen were putting down orange cones to warn people about a downed power line.

"Are you still here?" I called to the ghost. "Come out if you are."

I waited for him to reply. Just then a state trooper came by and "whooped" his siren as he passed through an intersection without stopping. The ghost sprinted around the corner of the building, terrified. "God, what is this place!?"

I caught his arm as he sailed by me and spun him around. He still had a "vibrating dough" feeling to him, but it didn't seem as strong as it had in the building. He drew back to hit me.

"Whoa," I said, holding up my hand in defense. "Settle down!"

Panting, he glanced past me to the fire truck's flashing lights.

"I am a lost soul," he whispered.

Even though I gripped his arm, my fingers weren't sinking in the way they had before. I looked down at his feet, and he stood solidly on the sidewalk just like I did.

"Let me see your hand," I said.

He gave me a blank stare. So I just pulled his arm up and took the bare flesh of his hand in mine. It was warm. I put my hand into his as if for a handshake. They did not merge as they had before. He was solid. I turned his hand over to examine the palm then put my fingers on his wrist. He had a pulse.

"You're alive," I said, surprised.

"Am I?" he asked in a relieved tone. "Are you certain?"

"You aren't a ghost," I said.

"This ain't perdition? I ain't passed over?"

"This is Kinsville," I said. "There are some here who might say it's perdition."

"This ain't Kinsville," he said. "I was just in Kinsville, and this ain't it."

10

"Let's go inside," I said.

"The building won't hold me," he said, shaking his head. "It's like it's made of fog or mud."

"It wasn't the building; it was you. But you're solid now. Look, I'm still holding your hand."

He gazed around at the parking lot and cars.

"Come on in," I said. "You can't stand out here dressed like that. People will have questions, and I don't think either one of us can answer them."

CHAPTER 3

When we stepped back inside the museum, he didn't sink. He stood just past the doorway and stomped his foot to test the floor.

"I think you're okay," I said.

He ignored me and stomped again then hopped up and down a couple of times. He was real. This was really happening.

"You're not a ghost, but I saw you appear out of thin air," I said.

He pulled the door shut then drew his revolver again.

"Don't," I said. "Please don't shoot me."

"I want some answers, you," he growled. "What place is this?"

"I told you where you were. Put the gun away."

"Where is my astra? I had it before. Did you take it?"

"I don't know what that is."

"I was caught in the floor and sinkin'. Did you do that to me?"

"Put the gun away," I insisted. "Something isn't right here, but let's talk about it. Maybe we can figure it out."

He stared at me warily then holstered his weapon.

"What's your name?" I asked.

12

"Soosen."

"Susan?" I grinned a little. "The girl name?"

"Soosen with two O's. Thaddeus Soosen," he frowned. "And yours?"

I extended my hand. "I'm Robert Bright. My dad runs this museum."

"Museum? Paintin's or curiosities?" He asked without shaking my hand.

"Historical exhibits," I replied.

"Hmph," he said.

"There was some lightning that struck the building. It lit up the floor just before you were there. I've never seen anything like it. I recall reading about ball lightning traveling into houses."

"'T'weren't lightnin'," he interrupted, "at least not how you think of it."

"I noticed your watch was glowing like the windows. Maybe the lightning struck you."

He looked down at his vest. The glow was gone, but he pulled his coat over the vest to hide it. He nodded again. "Must have opened an in-between," he said, distracted. "That's how that yellow devil got through."

I'd almost forgotten about the creature. "What was that thing?"

"That was a gurelach. It's from the other side."

"Other side of what?" I asked, exasperated. "Are you intentionally being vague? What's going on? Who are you? Where did you come from?"

"First you explain yourself. I am not yet certain you are a friend. Why do you dress in such an odd fashion? What were those machines and noises outside?"

Then I had an idea. "What year is it?" I asked.

His brow wrinkled, and he stroked his goatee. Finally, he said, "Eighteen hundred and seventy-seven. Every sane man knows that."

13

"And you were in Kinsville?"

He nodded and stared at me blankly, waiting for me to speak.

"Okay," I started, unsure what to say. "This is Kinsville—"

"It is not."

"It is. This is Kinsville, but...eighteen seventy-seven....that was like around..." I paused while I tried to do the math. "I don't know, maybe around a hundred and thirty or a hundred and forty years ago."

His blank stare lingered, and I couldn't read him.

"You are real and solid enough now," I continued, "so you aren't dead...you aren't a ghost. If you're telling the truth, then you are from another time. That can be the only explanation. It's crazy, but that must be it. Right?"

His hand went back to his goatee. "One hundred and forty years," he repeated.

"More or less."

"I'm slow to agree."

"You talk about yellow devils and in-betweens, but you can't accept time travel?"

"You have no understandin' in the matter," he said, wagging his head.

"Enlighten me."

He sighed. "With my Colt, I am, at best, able to defend against one more gurelach, and that is if my aim is true. I need the astra."

"What is it? What is an astra?"

He held his hands apart about ten inches. "It's about so long, shaped like a moon, and made of gold with a couple of blue jewels on the end. There is writin' on it."

"Gold? Nothing like that here."

"But I had it!" he snapped. "It was in my hand!"

"Not since I've seen you."

He huffed and stalked off into the other room.

14

"We have to leave," I called after him. "The police are closing the street!" Then I remembered the damage to the building. I needed to call dad so he could notify the insurance company, and I would need to get someone in to board up the windows until they can be repaired.

I went to dad's office to take care of these things. I found Soosen in the front gallery examining the displays.

"Those exhibits should be from your time period," I said as I opened the filing cabinet to retrieve the insurance information. Then I took a moment to appreciate what I had just said. This was living history, and my dad was missing it!

"It ain't here!" he said, irritated.

"I told you that," I replied as I scanned over the front page of the insurance form for a telephone number.

He moved into the gift shop.

"You sure won't find it in there," I said and pulled out my phone.

"Baubles and notions," he growled. He held up a foam can koozie with the picture of a horse and millstone on the side—the museum's logo. The original millstone had been kept in the museum's main gallery and often used as a display pedestal.

"Old Mill Museum," he read aloud, slowly pronouncing each syllable. He turned the can koozie over and over as if trying to determine its purpose, sniffed it then stuffed it into his coat pocket.

A time-travelling shoplifter.

My dad's phone went to voicemail, and I left a message.

"Are you talkin' to me?" The man called out. "Speak up!"

"No," I said. "Phone call."

"A what?"

I didn't try to explain what a phone call was. Instead, I called Carl, the handyman who serviced some of the non-profits in town. I got his voicemail too.

"Your thing isn't here," I said, exiting the office. "Come on; you can come home with me. We have a lot to talk about."

15

He dropped a plastic keychain into a bin and put his hands on his hips.

"We are in a grave time," he said with a frown. "I am obliged at your hospitality, but this is sore grave, this is. If there is one gurelach, there is bound to be more, if not now, then later. I think they'll come through here."

"Here in the building or here in town?"

"Near this place more like. That's where I came in."

I nodded, but I was still mostly clueless. "We can't stay here. *You* can't stay here."

"If the gurelach come through...." his voice trailed off, and his expression changed. He looked down at his feet, and his eyes widened. He was sinking again. He was losing cohesion fast. The blue glow had returned to his vest pocket. I rushed toward him with my hand outstretched, but he vanished.

CHAPTER 4

I stood over the spot in the floor where he'd disappeared and waited, but he never rematerialized. Perhaps I imagined or dreamed the whole thing. It would have been a stretch, but I was willing to make that stretch. Unfortunately, that drying glob of gurelach blood was still on my shoe, and I couldn't explain that away.

When I was sure Thaddeus Soosen would not return, I went into the office, removed the stained shoe, and held it close to my face to examine it.

There was a smell coming from it akin to ammonia. A thin film had dried over the top of the drop of blood. It was still soft underneath. It was thick, but not yet congealed. I wanted to save it. My friend, Lacy, was really good in biology. Maybe she could have a look at it. When she wasn't at school or working at her job at the Taco Barn, she volunteered at the hospital as a candy striper, and she was planning to go to nursing school.

Not finding anything in the office that would make a good specimen container, I went out to the gift shop and opened one of the empty plastic sports bottles, also with the horse an millstone logo and "Old Mill Museum" on the side, and scraped the blood into it. Out the window, I noticed the police

17

setting up sawhorse barricades in the street. I screwed the lid on the bottle, put my shoe on, and left.

There were some small limbs down on the road on my way home, but there was not as much debris as I thought there would be. I presumed the storm had fizzled before it moved toward my address. Carl returned my call as I was pulling in my driveway. I stressed to him the importance of safeguarding the exhibits from the outside elements, and he assured me he'd have the windows closed in with plywood before nightfall.

Our house and property, which was out in the county and away from town by at least five miles, showed no signs of damage. At worst, there had been a heavy rain there. I went inside. Salome, our two year old tabby, met me with a yowl. With dad gone for two weeks, the cat and I had the place to ourselves. My mom had died when I was young, and I had no siblings.

"Hey, Sal," I greeted her. "Are you hungry or just surprised to see me home so early?"

She curled around my leg and purred.

"Weird day," I said. "I'll change and tell you all about it."

I had to tell someone, and Salome wouldn't pass judgment on my honesty or sanity. Anyway, it wasn't like there was anyone else around to question my mental health for talking to the cat everyday like she was people.

I really needed a girlfriend.

Salome was unimpressed with the story, but it felt good to hear myself say it all out loud. When I finished, she licked her paw and rubbed it over her ear.

"I must have hit my head," I said. "It was a hallucination. I'll bet that drop of blood on my shoe was my own. It's just too crazy to believe."

She paused, stared at me then continued to clean herself. I immediately went into the bathroom to check my head in the mirror. I pushed my fingers through my hair, but didn't come across any wet or sore spots. Then my phone rang. I answered it with a distracted, "Hello?"

"Hey, Rob, did you make it through the storm okay?" It was Lacy.

"Yeah," I replied, still checking my head. "The museum took some damage."

"Is it bad? Did you call your dad?"

"Yeah, I called him." I paused and stared at my face. I wasn't an insane person. I wasn't injured. I had no other explanation I could fall back on.

"You okay?" she asked. "You sound off."

"Off how? Like crazy?"

"Huh? No. Were you hurt or something?"

"Don't think so."

"Maybe you should run by the E.R. and let them look you over."

"Don't they charge a lot at the E.R.?" I said. "Dad would freak."

"So you are hurt, and this is about saving your dad a few bucks."

"I didn't say that. I just had an odd day is all — too much stimuli."

"Are you home now or still at the museum?"

"Home," I replied.

"I'm coming over," she said flatly.

"Lacy, no, I'm fine I."

"I get off in half an hour. That gives you plenty of time to put some pants on."

I glanced down at my boxers and socks. She knew me too well. Salome had come into the bathroom and stood by my feet.

"Meow?" she said.

"Okay," I said to Lacy. "But really, I'm fine."

"Have you eaten? I'll get something."

"A pizza sounds good," I said.

19

"Yeah, but I get my employee discount on tacos. I'll see you in a few." She hung up.

"That was Lacy," I said to Salome as I put my phone back down next to the sink. "She's bringing tacos."

Lacy and I were pals since elementary school. When I was in third grade, my dad and I had just moved to town after he took the job at the museum, and I was the new kid. Even though I was a grade behind her, Lacy talked to me on the playground that first day and did her best to make me feel included.

Over the years, our friendship grew, but it had never escalated into something more. It's not that I didn't want it to, but I was afraid to tell her how I really felt about her. I was afraid it would make things awkward between us and drive her away. I couldn't bear the thought of not spending time with her, so we remained "just friends."

Lacy arrived an hour later, announced herself with a quick knock, then let herself in. She was still wearing her brown and orange uniform from the Taco Barn, and her dark hair was pulled back in a short ponytail. Neither the uniform, nor the hairstyle was very flattering, but even so, she couldn't help but be cute. She handed me the bag of tacos and picked up Salome.

"Hey, there Sally Mae," she said. "How's my girl?"

"I told you not to call her that," I said dryly. "You'll confuse her."

"Sally Mae is a country girl's name," Lacy said more to the cat than to me. "And this is a country girl if I ever saw one. But instead, your dad named her after an evil princess. Salome sounds too much like salami."

"Don't listen to her, Sal," I said.

She set the cat on the floor then took back the bag of tacos. "Before we eat, let me take a look at you."

"I'm fine."

"Did you hit your head?"

"No."

"No blurred vision or dizziness?" She stuck two fingers in front of my face and waved them back and forth. "We might need to get you to a doctor whether you want to or not."

"Stop it, Lacy," I said and pushed her hand away. "I'm fine. Come on, let's eat. Do you want a soda?"

"Okay," she shrugged with resignation. "At least tell me what happened. Were you in the building when the tornado came through?"

"Yeah," I replied on my way to the kitchen. "It blew the windows out, and lightning hit it."

"Those big old windows in front? That'll probably cost a fortune to replace."

"Yeah."

I wanted to tell her the rest, but I just couldn't bring myself to do it right then. Maybe after dinner....

CHAPTER 5

After two sodas, two tacos, and an hour and a half of TV, Lacy and I were lounging on the couch with Salome between us. I had been distracted the whole time by thoughts of what I had experienced, but I was no closer to telling Lacy about it than I had been before.

"If I gave you a blood sample, could you analyze it for me?"

She cut her eyes at me then chuckled. "Blood sample? From whom?"

"More like from what. I'm trying to identify what it came from."

She got a confused grin on her face. "What are you talking about?"

"I found some blood at the museum, and I'm curious about it. I put it in a plastic bottle for you."

At this she laughed, "For me? Rob, I'm not qualified for that. Why didn't you call the police if you were concerned about it?"

"You work in a hospital, don't you?" I said, irritated and embarrassed by her laughter. "You have access to labs, right? I didn't find much, just a drop of it."

"How do you even know it's blood? Maybe you spilled some tomato soup or something."

"That's why I wanted you to take it to the lab."

She shook her head, continuing to grin like it was a big joke. "It doesn't work like that. Can you see me sending a plastic bottle with a drop of tomato soup off to the lab? I'm not authorized to send any fluids to the lab, but even if I was, can you imagine how much trouble I would be in for wasting their time?"

"Never mind," I frowned.

"Oh don't get all sullen on me. I appreciate your faith in me, but I can't just go to the lab and run tests. Even if I had access, I wouldn't know what I was doing."

"Never mind," I repeated.

She stared at me a little longer than was comfortable.

Finally, she said, "Okay, give it to me, and I'll see what I can do."

"I don't want to get you into trouble," I said.

"Give it. I'm not promising anything, but there's a guy I know who might be able to get it through. He's asked me out a couple of times, so I think I could convince him."

"Who?" I asked, alarmed about this interloper and trying to act nonchalant.

"A new guy. He's a phlebotomist. I'd have to ask him about it."

"Phlegm-bottom-ist?" I said as casually as I could. "So is that like a special kind of doctor?"

She laughed again, "Phlebotomist. No, he draws blood. He can get it to the lab, but he really doesn't have much more authority than I do, so you might be out of luck. What's this all about?"

"I'll tell you later," I replied, "after I know for sure that it is blood and what kind."

"Now I'm intrigued."

"Never mind about it right now. I'll get the bottle, and you work your feminine wiles on Dr. Phlegm."

My phone rang.

23

"Hello?"

"Rob?" It was Carl the handyman.

"Hey, Carl, how are the windows coming along?"

"Tell your dad we got 'er closed up," he said. "It took six sheets of plywood, but we got 'er closed no problem."

"Good. Just send the bill."

"The main reason I called is I think an animal might have gotten into the building when it was opened up. We were just about to leave, and we heard a loud noise. We found one of the display cases knocked over. We couldn't find what did it, though. I'd look some more, but I can't stick around; the women's shelter lost part of their roof. I already sent the boys on ahead of me, but I need to get over there to help them. Do you want me to call animal control?"

I suspected my visitor had returned.

"No," I said. "I'll go back up there and look around. Just lock up. Thanks, Carl."

After I hung up, I stood.

"What's up?" Lacy said, not moving from her spot.

"The repair guy said he thinks something got into the museum through one of the broken windows. It knocked some stuff over. I'm going up there to have a look."

"Just call animal control," she said. "It's not worth it. It could be a rabid raccoon or possum."

"Probably just a cat," I said.

"Hear that, Sally?" Lacy said as she stroked Salome's head. "Daddy's going to go find you a friend." Then she stood. "I'll go help."

"No."

"No? Why not?"

"Um...no need. I can handle it," I said with a dismissive wave. "If it starts to feel dangerous, I'll call animal control."

She shrugged, "Okay. I guess I'll head home. I don't want my parents to send out a search party. Get me that blood sample." When she said "blood sample" she made air quotes with her fingers.

"It's over there," I said, pointing to the lamp table by the front door.

"The souvenir bottle?"

I nodded.

"Nice," she said and rolled her eyes.

I arrived at the museum just after seven that evening. Carl's tan truck was still parked in the back lot. I parked there next to it and went in through the back door, because the street on the front side of the building was still blocked off for work crews.

"Carl?" I called out. "You still here?"

There was no answer. I turned on the light and walked through the main gallery and into the smaller gallery and gift shop. The odor of the new plywood that covered the windows was obvious, but there was another more subdued smell in there too. It was ammonia.

"Carl?"

On an off chance, I ventured, "Thaddeus?"

The overturned display case was in the smaller gallery. It was the same exhibit the lightning had caressed earlier in the day. I moved to right it and check for damage to the items inside when I saw Carl's lace-up work boot sticking out behind another display farther in. He was on the floor.

"Carl? You okay?"

I found him in a puddle of blood. His throat had a gash, and there were six or seven evenly spaced holes in the side of his neck. He was pale. I checked his pulse. He was dead.

"No, no, no," I chanted as I backed away. I felt lightheaded. "Thaddeus? Thaddeus, are you in here?" I ran to the front door. There was still a police car parked about a block over, and I made for the blue lights.

"This can't be happening," I whimpered.

I knew what made those holes in his neck, and it wasn't a raccoon or cat. There was another gurelach, and I prayed it had not escaped the building.

CHAPTER 6

At nine o'clock that evening, they wheeled Carl's body to the back of the coroner's van on a stretcher. One of the city cops stood in front of me in his black uniform. He was listening to a report from a man from animal control.

"There ain't nothin' in there," the man said past a wad of snuff. "We can't find anywhere it coulda got in. If the bite was as big as you say, it would have to be a dog that did it." He took a second to spit. "Those windows are six feet off the ground at least, and dogs ain't gonna crawl up a buildin' like that to get in a window."

"What other explanation is there?" the policeman asked.

The man shrugged and spat, "I don't know, maybe a cougar, but they're rare around here, and I'd say you'd have a better chance of winnin' the Powerball jackpot than findin' a wild cougar in downtown Kinsville." The man finished in a low, suspicious tone. "Maybe it ain't an animal bite at all. Maybe somethin' else killed him. Maybe you should be searchin' for a murder weapon."

The cop grinned, "You worry about the dogs and possums. We'll worry about the two-legged animals."

The man spat and looked away, insulted.

Then another man walked over from the museum. He was in his late forties and his dark hair was graying at the temples. He wore a white dress shirt, tie, and a blazer. His paunch hung over the top of his dress slacks.

"Hey, Dan," he said and clapped the shoulder of the man from animal control. "How's the critter business."

The man smiled, "Oh, samo samo."

"How's Patty and the kids?"

"They're good. Rodney's plannin' to try for varsity this summer. He's workin' hard."

"That boy's a tank," the newcomer said with a big grin. "You tell everybody I said hey."

"Will do, Mr. Barnes."

After Dan from animal control walked away, the newcomer said to the uniformed cop. "Go ahead and give them a hand inside," he said, and the cop nodded, handed the man my driver's license, and walked away.

Then he turned to me and presented a badge. "I'm Detective Barnes. I'm with the Kinsville Police. I want to ask you a few questions."

"Okay," I said, "but the other guy already did that."

"I know, but I like to be thorough," he said and inspected my I.D. "Robert Bright," he read aloud. Then he looked up at me. "You just turned eighteen."

"Yes sir," I said. "Back in April."

"Did you go to Kinsville High? Do you know Dan's boy, Rodney?" he asked and hooked a thumb at the animal control guy.

"I know him," I said. "He was in my homeroom. We'll be seniors in the fall."

"That boy's a tank," he said with a big grin.

I didn't respond. I didn't really like Rodney very much.

"So you're still in school? You didn't graduate last month?"

"I got held back a year after my mom was sick. She died when I was seven."

"Sorry," he said and seemed to genuinely mean it.

I shrugged. "Thanks, but it was a long time ago."

"Are you related to Dr. Bright?"

"He's my dad. He's the museum director."

"Where is he?"

"He's out-of-town on business. I'm looking after things while he's gone."

"When do you expect him back?"

"He said he'd be back next Saturday. That's the thirteenth, I think."

"That long? I'll need to get in touch with him. Have you called him yet to let him know what's going on?"

"I called him this afternoon after the storm," I replied. "I left a message. I haven't called about this yet."

Then Detective Barnes spent the next few minutes asking me the same questions the other police officer had asked. When he was satisfied, he closed his little notebook. "You're free to go for now. We'll be in touch if we have any more questions."

He gave me a compassionate smile and put his hand on my shoulder. "Are you all right? I know what you saw in there was pretty gruesome. It might be difficult to deal with for someone your age."

"People my age go to war," I said.

"That's true, but that doesn't mean witnessing a violent death is any easier. I can recommend a counselor if you need to talk."

"Really, I'll be okay. What about the museum?"

"We're not done in there. We'd like another day at least to make sure we don't miss anything. Write down your dad's cell number, and I'll touch base with him."

"Dad will have the insurance company come look at the damage to the building," I said.

"They can wait a couple of days," he said. "We'll call you when we're done."

"But what if..." I almost mentioned the gurelach but stopped myself. "What if the animal comes back?"

"We hope it does so we can wrap this up. We'll have to put it down to keep it from hurting anyone else."

I nodded that I understood.

"When I call your dad, I am going to suggest he come home to be with you if he doesn't decide to do it on his own."

"No," I said. "Dad has enough stress on him right now. There's nothing he can do about any of this. This trip he's on could be the only thing that will save the museum from going under."

"Okay. I'll let you make that decision." Barnes handed me his card. "Here take this. If you can think of anything else we might need to know or if you need anything, give me a call."

When I got home, I called dad. As to be expected, he was upset.

"I'm gone for a few days, and everything falls apart. I'm catching the first plane out tomorrow."

"It would have happened whether you were here or not," I said.

"I know," he sighed. "I'm sorry. I wasn't trying to blame you. I just feel helpless so far away. I feel like I'm being irresponsible."

"There's nothing you can do. You finish your trip. Get the funding for the museum. I can keep things together here until you get back. I promise to give you updates every day, and I won't make any important decisions without your go ahead."

"I should at least come back for Carl's funeral."

"Sure, I guess," I said. "But that won't be for a few days, and I can let you know in plenty of time. I'd hate for you to cancel one of your meetings."

"I'll call his family in the morning and express my condolences."

"How is the trip going?"

"I'm not having any luck out here," he said. "Any one of these foundations could write us a check to cover our budget for a whole year, and they'd never miss the money. They just don't think we're important. They keep telling me Kinsville is too small for a museum like ours. I wasn't expecting to hit so many walls."

"Don't give up and don't stress. All you need is one good patron to get us through another year. If all else fails, we can bring in the Sasquatch fur."

"I hate to admit it, but we might have to resort to one of your outlandish gimmicks just to keep the doors open. Have you heard from anyone on the museum's board of directors yet?"

"No," I said. "I figured they would have called *you* after the storm."

"They don't have my cell phone number. If they want to reach me, they can E-mail me or wait until I get back. I won't be able to talk to all of them individually for a few days. I don't expect any problems from then; they're usually supportive. If anyone causes a stink over all of this, it'll be Edith Haber. She's on the city council, and she's been pushing to cut the city's funding of the museum for years."

"Yeah, I've met her before," I said.

"She wants us gone. I think she has plans for the building or something. She's a pest. Don't let her push you around. If she calls or drops by, just tell her I will contact her as soon as my schedule permits. If she won't leave you alone, give Dr. Randolph a call at the university. He's on the museum board, and he can run interference for you."

"Okay," I said. "I did give your cell number to the police. I hope that was all right."

"Of course," he said. "I would like to talk to them. I have already contacted the insurance company about the storm damage, and I instructed them to call me back about that."

"Don't stress out, dad. I got this."

He paused before he spoke again, trying to hold back tears. "I'm proud of you, son. You are shaping up to be a fine man. You've had to grow up so fast, and you graduate next year, then you're off to college. I don't know what I'll do without you. Two big accidents happened at the museum today. I could have lost you today. I don't have to tell you the past few years have been tough without your mom."

"Stop it, dad. I've got your back. You get some rest then go out tomorrow and sweet talk one of those rich dudes out of some of their money."

"I hope you don't feel like I am pressuring you. I hope I haven't put too much on you. How have you been doing anyway? Have you been thinking much about college? Is Lacy still planning to stay local and commute?"

"Yeah, Lacy is going to go to school close by," I said. "I don't know about college. I haven't thought about it much."

"You've always had a love for history like your old man, but I can't say I would recommend the museum end of it. Maybe archaeology or maybe a professorship would be a more stable career choice. There are two colleges within driving distance that have decent programs."

"I don't know. Maybe I'll take a year off. Maybe I'll join the army. I don't really like school much anyway."

He was quiet for a bit, "Okay. I don't want to pressure you. It's your life. It's just that you're already a year older than the rest of your class. You're already a year behind. I hope this isn't about money. You can apply for financial aid."

It was about money. He didn't have the money to pay my tuition, and I was neither a good enough student, nor athletic enough to get a scholarship. "We can talk about it when you get back."

"Okay. Love you, Robbie."

"Love you too. Bye."

I wanted to call Lacy and tell her all about Carl. I wanted to tell her about all of it, including the time traveler and the monster, but I didn't know how. I took a hot shower then sat in front of the TV with Salome snoozing in my lap. A *Friends* rerun was on, but I didn't really watch it. I couldn't sleep; I was too wired. Then a muddled memory flashed into my head — something I'd read in a scan from an old newspaper.

"Eighteen seventy-seven," I said aloud. Salome cracked open an eye. "He was from eighteen seventy-seven!" I stood quickly, and the cat landed on her feet in the floor with her ears back. "There were some odd deaths around the town about that time," I mumbled to myself.

I moved over to the computer desk. There were digital copies of Kinsville's old newspapers at the museum, but I wouldn't be able to get in there for at least a day.

"Maybe the library has their files available online," I said.

They did not.

"Well, it was worth a shot, Sal. I guess I'll be visiting the library tomorrow."

Then I did a web search for "Thaddeus Soosen." There was no record of anyone by that name during the late 1800's. I tried spelling it different ways but still no luck. Then I tried searching for the two words he had mentioned — gurelach and astra — spelling them as best as I could. I found nothing on "gurelach" no matter how I spelled it, but "astra" did come up.

"'A weapon of great power and supernatural origin," I read out loud. "In Hindu mythology, these weapons were guarded by deities who would release them only for specific purposes and only to those who possessed the knowledge of their use.' Wow. How about that, Sal?"

Salome had one leg in the air and was licking herself.

"A time traveler searching for a magical weapon so he can kill demons," I said. "I think I need to get some sleep so I can wake up from this nightmare."

33

I did sleep that night, but not much. Lacy woke me with a phone call just before 8 A.M.

"Hello?"

"God, you're alive! I just watched the morning news," she shouted in my ear. "Are you kidding me?! Somebody died at the museum and you didn't call me?! When I saw the story, I thought it was you!"

"I was going to call you, but I knew you had to go to work in the morning."

"They said he was probably killed by a rabid dog," she said. "I told you it could have been dangerous. You should have called animal control from the beginning."

"I know."

"Does this have anything to do with that water bottle you sent home with me?"

I sighed, "Yeah. I mean, I think so."

"Did you tell the police? Did you tell them you found blood?"

I lay there in bed staring at the ceiling for a moment. Finally, I admitted, "No."

"Rob! What are you doing? What is going on?"

"I don't know."

"Did you know him? Did you know that man that was killed? They didn't give his name."

"It was Carl," I said. "The guy that called me last night."

"Oh, I'm sorry."

I held the phone for a few seconds. "I need to talk to you when you get a chance."

"I have a chance now. Why do you think I called?"

"No, not on the phone. I need to talk to you in person. Something happened yesterday, and you are the only one I can tell right now."

"Why didn't you talk about it yesterday? Are you in trouble?"

"I don't know."

"I'm supposed to volunteer at the hospital today," she said. "I have to be there at nine, but I'll call in sick."

"No, don't call in or anything. Just do me a favor and talk to your friend about that blood. It is really important. Can you meet me after you get off?"

"Are you going to the museum?"

"No," I replied. "The police are still there. I plan to go to the library then I'll be home the rest of the day."

"Pick up something for dinner, and I'll be by when I get off," she said in a solemn tone. "You're worrying me, Rob."

"Everything is okay," I said, trying to sound convincing. "I'll see you later."

When I ended the call, it immediately rang again. The caller I.D. said it was Edith Haber, the woman dad warned me about from the city council. I groaned and let it go to voicemail.

CHAPTER 7

I arrived at the library not long after it opened that morning at 9 o'clock. The regulars were there—four old men in the periodicals section, legs draped, faces hidden behind newspapers. I nodded a greeting to the woman behind the desk and found a computer in the back where I could access their digital archives. I had volunteered at the library with my dad a couple of years before to help them scan some of their old microfilm and microfiche to a digital format. It was still ongoing, and they had people who worked on the project a few hours each month. They were always gracious enough to give copies of the scans to the museum when sets were completed.

I didn't find the digital versions easy to navigate—for me, the microfilm was faster—but at least archives were preserved and protected, and the information in them would last forever.

In 1877, there were two different newspapers operating in Kinsville, The Democrat and The Monitor, both long defunct. Fortunately for me, they were both weekly publications rather than daily; it would make my task of going through them a little easier. They weren't really like the newspapers we have now; they only had two pages—one sheet printed front and back. The print was tiny, and the stories were crammed together. There were no pictures at all. I moved through the pages quickly reading only the headlines.

Both papers had missing issues, which was to be expected with something so old, but most of the holes left by either paper were filled by the other. After all, they were competing press covering the same news in the same small town, so I was sure a sensational story like the one for which I was searching would have been reported by both.

The Monitor lacked the last three weeks of April 1877, but The Democrat had it covered. That is where I found the first story. It was in the fourth week of April. A family had been killed at their farm. William and Charlotte Hanes and their young daughter, Polly, were "massacr'd whilst they slept," the paper said. They had been dead for several days before they were discovered by a neighbor. The story went on to say, "...negro, Jacob Massey, has been taken to the jail under suspicion."

There was no more mention of Mr. Massey's fate in subsequent issues, but other stories about more strange deaths popped up in the second and third week of May and the first week of June. The first case in May was blamed on bandits, but by June, all four cases, including the Hanes family, had been changed to suspected wolf attacks. I found it odd that the authorities at the time would even suggest a wolf since wolves had been driven out of the state decades before. Then, toward the bottom of the story it said, "...bite marks on their lifeless forms."

"Bite marks," I whispered.

The story finished by saying a hunt was to be organized and that citizens should "keep a rifle at the ready."

I was just about to load the July issues on the computer when my phone rang. The old men at the periodicals table frowned in my direction. I waved an apology and answered it quietly without actually whispering.

"Yes?"

"Is this Robert Bright?" said the caller.

The woman at the front desk glowered and pointed at a sign that said, "PLEASE TAKE CELL PHONE CALLS OUTSIDE."

"Are you there?"

"Yes," I hissed into the phone and got up to go outside.

"This is Detective Barnes with the Kinsville Police Department. We spoke last night. I have a man here who says you know him. He claims to be a Mr. Soosen."

"Soosen!" I said way too loudly. The entire population of the library shushed me. I waved another apology just as I stepped outside the building. "Thaddeus Soosen?"

"Yes," the detective replied. "So you know him? He doesn't have any I.D. on him, and we found him in the building. If he hadn't been dressed in old-timey clothes, I would have arrested him. I figured he had something to do with the museum being dressed like that."

"Yes," I said, trying to think of a plausible thing to say. "I've been expecting him. He's.... um...he's a reenactor my dad hired."

"Reenactor? Like the Civil War stuff?" Detective Barnes sighed heavily into the phone and continued. "Robert, we have the whole museum taped off for the investigation. It's like that for a reason. We can't have your dad's reenactors stopping in like this. I didn't want to take him in, but he's not being very cooperative."

"No! Don't do that," I said. "He's...he's probably just trying to stay in character; those reenactors do that. He doesn't mean any harm. He's from out-of-town, and he's going to help us with a fundraiser. I'm at the library. I'll be right over to pick him up."

I ended the call and ran out to my car. So long as Mr. Soosen didn't disappear again, I could get information from him that those old newspapers could not give.

I found Thaddeus Soosen sitting on the front steps of the museum unchaperoned. He hugged his knees and took in his surroundings with wide eyes, somehow subduing the hysterics he undoubtedly felt from exposure to this modern, alien world.

I parked my car in the lot and got out. He didn't move except to rock in place a little. I stepped away from the car so he could see my whole form.

"The young Mr. Bright," he called to me.

He stood, but made no effort to approach me. Then the door of the museum opened, and Detective Barnes stepped out.

"Good morning, Robert," the detective said.

"Hi. How are things going inside?"

"We're going as fast as we can. So, you know this man?"

"Yes," I replied. "He's doing some work for the museum."

"Right," Barnes said, but his tone said "Liar."

I felt uncomfortable under his scrutiny so I turned back to Thaddeus. Detective Barnes went back inside and shut the door, but he watched us through the door's window.

"This world of yours is a might loud and vexed," Thaddeus said. He pointed at my car. "These....things—are they carriages?"

"Yes," I shrugged. "Are you hungry? I'll take you to my house."

He looked over his shoulder at the museum one more time then walked over to me.

"I need to be in your shop," he said in a low tone. "The coppers forced me out, but I am certain my way back is inside."

"You disappeared before," I said when he stopped in front of me. "Where did you go?"

"Back to Kinsville," he said. "But only for a time."

"You're in Kinsville now," I said.

"So you say."

I went to the passenger door of the car and opened it like a chauffeur.

"Get in and sit," I said.

He stared into the car and frowned, "Must I?"

"If you want to go home with me, you must."

"I want to go to *my* home."

"That can't be done right now," I said. Detective Barnes still stood at the museum's door. "If you don't go with me, the police might take you in."

"Take me in?"

"Jail," I replied.

"I don't wish for jail, but...." his voice tailed off as he continued to stare into the car.

"It's comfortable in there," I said in a reassuring tone.

"I am afraid," he admitted and dropped his eyes.

"Trust me," I said. "I'm a friend."

Finally, he gripped the top of the car and put his foot in on the seat. I almost laughed—getting into a car should be a simple thing—but I kept my composure.

"Would you like me to show you how?" I asked.

He pulled his foot from the vehicle, puffed his chest out, and turned to face me. He gave the bottom of his vest an indignant tug to straighten the wrinkles from the fabric.

"I am a capable man, sir. I think you should get into this machine before me. I need assurance this is not a trap."

"No problem," I grinned. "But I'll need to get in on the other side. You can watch if you want."

He watched me walk around the vehicle. I opened the driver's side door. His eyes narrowed, studying me. Slowly, I sank below the roofline of the car. When I slid into the driver's seat, he scrutinized my every move. I shut the door and pulled the seatbelt over and clicked it.

"Why the lashing?" he asked.

"Huh? Oh, the seatbelt. It's for safety."

"Safety," he said in a doubtful tone.

"Climb in, Mr. Soosen."

40

CHAPTER 8

I had hoped the ride home would be full of enlightening conversation, and I would be able to at least begin my interview of this man, this time traveler. It didn't work out that way.

One must keep in mind that prior to strapping into my Honda that morning, the fastest speed Thaddeus Soosen had experienced was on horseback—probably no more than 40 miles per hour, and only for a short distance. Even the steam locomotives of his time rarely reached 30 miles per hour. Our sustained speed of 60 in my car was a completely new experience for him.

"Everlasting God!" he screamed as I blew past a man on a bicycle. Thaddeus' knees were around his ears and his boots were pressed against the dashboard.

"It's okay," I said. "I promise. See? Look at me."

He cut his eyes over at me. "Satan is a deceiver."

"No," I said calmly. "I'm not Satan. It's me: Robert Bright. We're going to my house. We'll have sandwiches. Please take your feet down. If the airbag goes off, you'll wish you'd listened to me."

A car approached in the opposite lane at a similar speed. Soosen pushed his fists into the ceiling. "Eternal God!"

41

"Really," I said. "It's okay."

That went on all the way home. Thankfully, it wasn't far. When we arrived at home, he was gasping for air. I helped him with his seatbelt then walked around to open his door. He rolled out of the car and to my gravel driveway on hands and knees. I bent and grabbed his elbow to help him up. He came up fast, and before I could respond, he smacked my jaw with the back of his hand.

I yelped and dropped to one knee.

"What was that for?" I said, holding my face.

"I thought it unwise to do it while you were steering the carriage. So I waited until we stopped."

"Um....thank you?" I said as I stood again.

We frowned at each other.

"Do you still want to eat?" I asked finally.

He removed his hat and bowed slightly. "I am grateful for your hospitality."

We walked up the sidewalk to my front door. Everything, from the concrete under our feet, to the vinyl siding on my house, to the metal storm door was inspected and touched by the newcomer. Inside, he acted the way Salome had when dad brought her in for the first time. He cowed and skulked and investigated everything in the living room.

"I suppose a lot of what you see here is foreign to you," I said as I took food from the refrigerator.

He picked up one of Sal's toys from the floor—an orange, furry, fake mouse. He sniffed it then put it in his pocket.

"Put it back," I said. "That's her favorite one."

"Pardon?"

"The toy mouse. Put it back, and please don't take anything else."

"Are you callin' me a thief?"

"You put that mouse in your pocket," I said. "And I saw you steal that item in the gift shop too."

"You insult me and my honor," he said.

42

"You insult *me*!" I shot back. "You are a guest. I don't know how honorable men acted in eighteen seventy-seven, but nowadays, men of honor don't steal."

We glared at each other a moment then he reached into his pocket and pulled out the mouse. He held it up for me to see, gave me a quick smart-ass smile then dropped it on the floor. He reached into his pocket a second time and, with a flourish, produced the koozie and dropped it next to the mouse.

"Thank you," I said. The living room was full of strange objects, modern gadgets, and books. That was a lot of temptation. "Tell you what," I said, "why don't you have a seat. I don't think you should be looking at or touching anything else. It might mess up the fabric of time or something. The less you know about the future, the better."

"Fabric?"

"Please," I replied. "Just sit."

He removed his hat then sat on the sofa. I kept an eye on him while I finished making his sandwich, but he didn't move from that spot. A couple of minutes later, I entered the living room with a plate of food and offered it to him.

"Mr. Robert Bright," he said in a formal and dignified voice, "I cannot recall havin' ever sat on a more fluffy bench. It is a joy to my backside. My compliments."

"Yeah," I said. "Sure. Here, eat up."

He took the plate and examined the food.

"It's ham and cheese on rye," I said.

"I am grateful," he said.

I took a seat in my desk chair and stared at him. There was a man from the Victorian Era sitting in my living room balancing a ham sandwich plate on his lap. I had so many questions.

"Tell me about yourself, Mr. Soosen."

He picked up his sandwich, smelled it, and tried a nibble.

"Not much to tell," he said. "You know my name already."

"Are you from Kinsville originally?"

He shook his head and took a larger bite of the sandwich, "No."

"Just passing through?"

"No."

I tried again.

"How old are you?"

"I am twenty and eight years old."

I did the math.

"So you remember the war," I said, referring to the Civil War.

"Remember it?" he chuckled. "Yes, I do at that."

"You were just a child then, I suppose."

He shook his head. "I was a fightin' man."

"You were only in your early teens when the war began."

"I was old enough," he said. Then he cocked his head and held up the sandwich. "I relish this food."

"And your allegiance during the war?"

He regarded me with suspicion. "I was and am for the continued union of these United States."

"But Kinsville was a Confederate town," I said. "In fact, it was sort of a Confederate hotbed for this region, wasn't it?"

"I have dealin's in Kinsville that have nothin' to do with the rebellion," he said coldly. "I trust that you and I can put aside our standin's. The war has been over for many years. I try not to hold grudges, but if you do, we can deal with that now." He opened his jacket away from his revolver.

"I have no grudge or stand," I said. "For me, that war happened so long ago it is almost irrelevant."

"Irrelevant?" He snapped, anger flashing in his eyes. "Irrelevant," he said again as if the word tasted bad. "Mr. Bright, have you ever brought a man to his end? Have you ever watched a man's eyes die whilst you squoze his throat or slid a knife in his ribs?"

I just shook my head.

44

"Those men and I had differin' minds on the matter of our union, but they were men. Whatever their age, they were men. They looked like me. They had women back home that cried for them—mothers and sisters and daughters and wives. They were brave and unlucky, but they were not irrelevant. If what you say is true, Mr. Bright, and I am in a different time, then you are the irrelevant one. You are the one who hasn't happened yet."

"I meant no offense," I said. "I apologize."

He nodded and took another bite of the sandwich.

"What is your business in Kinsville?" I asked.

He stopped chewing for a moment then resumed without a reply.

"A man died last night," I added.

"Your coppers said as much."

"And? He had bite marks. You understand?"

Soosen was visibly alarmed when I mentioned the bites. Then he said, "I am sworn not to speak of it."

"But I've already seen it! That monster almost fell on me!"

"That is a sorry turn," he admitted. Then he thought it over and added, "I reckon I can lend you insight. Ain't no one will ever believe your tales if you tell it. But I must return to your shop once the coppers are gone. The astra must be there. My way back home should be there as well."

"What is the 'in-between'? That's what you said yesterday."

He paused and looked away as if trying to come up with the right words. Finally, he said, "It's like a threshold. There are these gates. They ain't like real gates, but they work the same. You can't see them, but they open up and allow passage from one world to another. We call the passage the 'in-between,' because when one goes through, they exist neither in this world, nor the next."

"How do the gates open?"

"Sometimes they open by themselves because of Earth's movement through the heavens, but there are keys that can open the gates whenever a person fancies. I reckon I must be here because of a key, though I cannot recollect usin' it."

"These other worlds, are they different planets?"

"Not like that. It is the same planet, but different worlds on that planet. There are thirteen primary worlds—seven are the Octave worlds and six are the Gradi worlds. There are also many worlds between, but they are differin' versions of the thirteen. Earth is the central world, like the hub of a wagon wheel. Yet, all the worlds exist in the same place."

"Do you mean other dimensions? You traveled in time."

"I am not certain what you mean by 'other dimensions'. I did not know one could move through time until I did it."

"Okay," I said, but I didn't really grasp what he told me. "And the demon? What is a gurelach?"

"They come from a place called Jeoke," he said with a mouth full of sandwich. "It's a world on the lower plane. I am to kill them when I see them. That is all I know. That is all I aim to say." He swallowed then shoved the remainder of his meal into his mouth.

"Okay," I said. "What about your watch? Why did it glow before you disappeared?"

He placed his hand over his vest pocket, but he did not pull out the watch. He was perplexed.

"Did it glow?"

"Yeah, didn't you notice?"

I started to speak again, but he lifted a hand, and shook his head. I waited for him to swallow so he could speak. Finally he said, "I can see you are a kind young man, and I feel most obliged for your care for me durin' this time, but I am sworn not to talk on these things. I have said more than I ought. I don't aim to tell you more."

I frowned.

Then he said, "We can ruminate on other matters."

He wasn't going to tell me about other worlds and monsters. That was disappointing, I tried to appreciate that there was a man from the Victorian Era sitting on my couch. My dad would have loved to have a chance to interview a veteran of the Civil War. I had a great idea. I went to the computer at the desk in the living room and set the webcam to record. Then I turned to Thaddeus.

"Tell me about your time in the war," I said. "Don't leave anything out."

CHAPTER 9

"I left home two days before Christmas in sixty-three. I knowd I hurt my momma in doin' it, but I couldn't sit by while others sacrificed. My brother fell at Sharpsburg the year before, and momma grieved over him every day. I'd planned on stayin' by her until the new year, but when I heard tell that Burnside and his men were in Tennessee, I didn't want to wait. I left straight away and j'ined up with General Sturgis there at Mossy Creek." Soosen paused and shook his head. "I was so green and innocent, fourteen years old, hungry for revenge and glory." He frowned at me, "There ain't nothin' glorious about killin' men, and revenge ain't as satisfyin' as it orta be. And those men there that day....well, I 'spect they weren't directly responsible for George's death."

"Was George your brother?"

He nodded.

"Go on," I said.

"Sturgis sent Colonel LaGrange to Dandridge to take a rebel camp, and I was part of that, but we didn't find no rebs there. I admit to you, by the time we arrived, I was all tore up inside and relieved to see they'd gone. I felt cowardly about it back then, but I know now that bein' afraid and bein' a coward ain't the same."

He stopped talking and his gaze was a thousand miles away.

"What happened?" I asked.

He continued to stare, "A messenger rode in with urgent orders for us to return to Mossy Creek. The rebels had moved in on our camp there, comin' in from two sides. We rushed back to help, and I got my first taste of fightin'. I saw many men die that day. I took my first life. He was a man of middle years—old enough to be my pa. He was braver than I; he didn't cry none. I have since made up tales about him in my head, and in my stories, he was a fine man with a comely daughter, and I like to think that in a different circumstance, she and I were married, and he gave his blessin'. That's the story I tell in my head when the weight of his passin' presses in on me."

There was an awkward silence, so I steered my questions to historical interests.

"Refresh my memory—was this all a part of the Knoxville Campaign? Did you ever meet General Burnside?"

"We were nigh to Knoxville," Soosen replied. "I don't know about campaigns; that's the talk of officers. I did see Burnside at a distance, but I never had the pleasure of his acquaintance. Impressive whiskers, that man. Such influence that it became the fashion....but not for me; I prefer my beard to be orderly." Then he grinned and gave me a wink, "I think the ladies do too."

"How many battles were you in?"

"There was fightin' and killin' over the next few months, but I never saw nothin' like what George saw at Sharpsburg. Then, in the early summer of sixty-four, the war ended for me. I was accused of lootin' a house and killin' the man that owned it. The sergeant had me shackled, and hauled me back to camp to let the captain decide my fate."

"Did you do it?"

49

"I took a few pretties from the house as presents for my momma, but the man was already dead when I got there. The sergeant shackled me, and I stayed shackled until that night. That's when I was taken."

"Captured?"

"Kidnapped," he replied but changed his mind. "No, I was rescued. Men came into camp in the night and took me. It was for the best."

"How? I don't understand. Men just came into camp and took you? Where did they take you? Did you fight back? Didn't anyone help you?"

"I fought, but they were stronger. I thought they was gonna lynch me. They came in quiet, and they kept *me* quiet. Even without the charges against me, you have to understand that it was commonplace for men to desert or go home for a time to tend to family. I 'spect when it was discovered I was missin', they just figured I had escaped or turned tail. It pains me to be thought of as a coward, but as I said, it was for the best."

"Who took you? If you weren't captured by the Confederacy, then who was it?"

"It was a conscription of sorts. I was chosen to work for someone who needed a man like me."

"What sort of work? You were just a boy!"

"I was young, but that wasn't to my hurt. I wasn't beyond learnin'. They believed me to be a thief and a killer, and I let them think it. They knew I had a momma in need and—"

"Did they threaten her?" I asked.

"They offered a good life for me and her. All I had waitin' for me if I had gone back to the war was a noose or a bullet. If I did, through some miracle, make it home, there was thirty-two acres of poor, rocky ground waitin' for me."

There was a noise outside, and I was jerked away from the conversation. "Excuse me a sec," I said. Through the window, I spied Lacy coming up the sidewalk. I groaned.

"What is it?" Soosen asked.

"Lacy," I said, pulling up the blinds. "She's a friend, but she doesn't need to see you. Maybe you should stay out of sight until I get rid of her. I haven't told her about you yet."

"Where shall I go?" he asked. "Why not tell her what you told the coppers—that I am here in masquerade?"

There was a quick knock and Lacy came in. She was wearing her pink scrubs—her candy striper uniform. "I hope you are dressed!" she called out with a laugh then was startled to find Soosen and I on the other side of the room staring at her.

"Oh....hello?" she said.

Thaddeus Soosen stood, holding his hat over his heart. Then he bowed and approached her with an outstretched hand. Lacy lifted her own, expecting a handshake, but instead, Soosen took her fingers gently, and kissed her just above the knuckles.

"Thaddeus Soosen, ma'am," he said.

"Huh?" she said, now more startled than before. She cut her eyes over to me for clarification.

"It's his name," I said.

"Oh," she said. "Lacy. I'm Lacy."

"Enraptured," was Soosen's reply. He continued to hold her hand and grin.

I rolled my eyes. "Mr. Soosen is...." I didn't want to lie to her, but I wanted to wait until Lacy and I were alone to tell her the full story. "Mr. Soosen is helping out with some facts about local history."

"For the museum?" she asked in a dreamy voice.

"Sure" I said. "Why are you here? I thought we were getting together this evening."

"Why are you dressed like that?" she asked Thaddeus.

"Steampunk cosplay?" I ventured.

"What's that?" The two said in unison.

"Never mind. Aren't you supposed to be at the hospital?"

51

"I'm on my lunch break. I was worried about you," she said, but her eyes were still locked with Soosen's.

"To be cared for by a woman is a coveted thing," Soosen cooed. "Especially by one so lovely." He lifted her hand again for a second kiss.

"Cut it out," I said.

Then, like before, he began to fade. The blue glow had returned to his vest pocket. He still held Lacy's hand, and she was fading too.

"Rob? What's happening?" Lacy screamed, her eyes wide.

"No!" I yelled. I went to grab her. My fingers brushed her arm, and I felt a prickling. I stretched and managed to take hold of Thaddeus' coat.

I heard a strong wind then my living room and its contents transformed into vibrating blue light.

CHAPTER 10

The blue light energy changed to a cool, clear mist, but it wasn't wet. A rushing wind buffeted us. My living room was gone. There was still a tingle in the air like static electricity and an odor of ammonia. The three of us had not moved in relation to each other, but our environment had changed and was continuing to change every second or two. In the mist, transparent rooms and landscapes appeared and disappeared around us like projections in the fog. Some of these places were occupied by people or animals, and we went unnoticed by them.

Thaddeus was as alarmed as I. Unsure what to do, I continued to hold onto him.

"What is this?!" Lacy screamed. "What's happening?!"

"It ain't right!" Thaddeus replied over the roar of the wind. "Ain't been like this before!"

"Before?" Lacy said. "This happened before?"

Around us was a forest...no...

a meadow with a stone wall...

a gray desert with a small dome in the distance...

a small room littered with broken pottery....

The fleeting environments might have been real, but they were not solid. A few times, I occupied the exact same space as an object or person. As the scenes changed, I felt funny in my stomach as though I was riding an elevator.

Mingled in the wind, there was chatter like hundreds of voices speaking at once. The stench of ammonia worsened. Then, in an instant, gurelachs were everywhere.

Startled, the three of us cried out and covered our faces as the creatures attacked.

They leapt and writhed, slashed and gnashed, but they could not touch us. Like the shifting scenes around us, they lacked sufficient substance to make contact. They even passed through our bodies. Although they could not physically harm me in this state, I still felt them. They were cold, and there was something like a wave of sadness or depression that would wash through me when the monsters and I shared the same space.

To each other, however, they were quite solid. There were collisions and fights among them, and I even noticed black blood oozing from the injured.

"Scores of 'em!" Thaddeus wailed. He was down in a crouch covering his ears. "Ain't never seen so many!"

Lacy panicked and screamed. She thrashed and twisted, batting at the gurelachs with one hand as if she'd just walked through a spider web. With the other hand, she still held tight to Thaddeus'.

I let go of Thaddeus, then like closing up an airtight room to a hurricane, the roaring wind slurped to silence, and I was back in my living room....alone.

"No, no, no...Lacy? Thaddeus? Lacy!?"

Then my phone rang.

"Hello?"

"Rob, thank God you're okay! I had no idea if you would answer. Are you at home? Where are you?"

"Lacy? What the—?"

54

"I'm at the museum. Can you come pick me up?"

"I don't understand. You were just here."

"I don't know how to explain it. I'll tell you in person. I'll be waiting."

After the events of the past couple of days, that phone call did not shock me. It was unexpected but not shocking. I left immediately and drove to the museum, before the police could give her trouble about being there the way they had with Thaddeus.

I found her sitting on the curb next to the building. She no longer wore her pink uniform, but was instead clothed in a drab ochre dress with frilly sleeves. Black lace-up boots had replaced her brightly-colored nursing shoes. She was sweaty and dirty, and her hair was a mess. I pulled over and parked on the street.

"Are you okay?"

"I'm back," she said. "I'm glad you're safe. We were worried you had been taken by the monsters."

"Where did you go?" I asked. "Where is Thaddeus?"

"I don't know where he is. I was hoping he would show up."

"Are you hurt?"

She checked herself and shook her head. "No. I don't think so. We have to find him. It's important."

"Where did these clothes come from?"

"I had to change," she said. "I had to fit in. We burned my other clothes so no one would find them."

"You were only gone for a few seconds," I said.

"Longer....almost two whole days. Was it only seconds here? I was here—right here in this very spot—but it was eighteen seventy-seven."

"Eighteen seventy-seven."

"It's crazy, Rob. This is all crazy. Why didn't you tell me? Thaddeus said he told you everything. Why did you keep it from me?"

"He didn't tell me everything," I said. "Anyway, I didn't know if I was losing my mind until this morning when he came back. I planned to tell you. I didn't think you'd believe me."

"We're friends," she said as she stood and smoothed out her dress. "Of course I'd believe you....or at least I'd believe that you believed it."

My phone rang. I checked it. "Ugh. Edith Haber again." I forced it to go to voicemail. "What did the police say about you being here?"

"They don't know I'm here," she replied. "I just sort of dropped in right here next to the building. I was going to go inside, but the police cars are still here and it was still taped off." She paused and let out a heavy breath. "The past two days have been....wow."

"Tell me," I said. "Come on. Let's go back to my house."

"But what if he comes back?"

"He could come back at my house. I did."

She shrugged and got in the car.

Right as we got underway, she reached down the front of her dress, dug around in her cleavage, and fished out her phone. "I have pictures."

My breath caught. "Pictures," I whispered.

Actual cell phone pictures of 1877 Kinsville! To my knowledge, only 3 non-portrait photographs from Kinsville even existed prior to 1895. These would be like treasure for my dad. Lacy tapped and swiped at her phone, then handed it to me.

"Careful looking," she said. "Don't wreck."

The first image was of two small clapboard buildings with wooden shingles—one white, the other unpainted—next to a dirt path. There was a hitching post between them, and a horse was tied to it. Behind those two buildings was the gristmill.

"The museum," I said. "I almost didn't recognize it. There was an addition added to it later where those other buildings are, and the roof is different."

"Those two buildings in front were a blacksmith shop and a stable," she said.

I swiped to the next picture. It was of a narrow dirt road with deep ruts. Several buildings lined it on both sides. There were people there too.

"That picture is of what is now West Broadway. It wasn't all dirt. Part of it was paved with bricks."

I swiped back to the first picture of the mill again. "Amazing," I said. "I had no idea. I've seen old maps of the period, but not everything was labeled."

"You wouldn't have known it anyway. Without all the landmarks, it's almost impossible to tell. The only reason I knew where we were was because Thad knew and pointed it out for me. Do you think he'll follow me back?"

"I don't know," I said. "Did you just call him Thad? That's kind of familiar, don't you think?"

"He said I could. What's wrong with it?"

The phone made an odd beeping noise.

"Battery is almost gone," she said and took it from me. "I need to charge it. I'll send the pictures to you later." She pulled her collar and dropped the phone back inside.

"That dress is something," I said.

"I know it's ugly, but it was all we could find."

"No," I said. "I think you look nice."

She snorted. "I'm a mess. I'm dirty, I smell, and this shade of yellow is not flattering at all."

"I think it's nice," I said. "It's a little frumpy, maybe, but I'm used to seeing you in your work clothes or jeans. The last time I saw you in a dress was the homecoming dance. You looked really pretty that night."

She shook her head and chuckled. "Ugh, homecoming. I can't believe I agreed to go with Rodney to that thing."

"Yeah," I frowned. "I can't either."

57

"You and I should have gone together. If I had known you didn't have a date, I would have suggested it. I hated to see you be a wallflower."

"The person I wanted to go with already had a date," I said.

"Well, too bad for her," she said and patted my leg.

"So tell me what happened with Thaddeus," I said, changing the subject. "Those things were all over us then I came back to my living room. You called me less than a minute later."

"I saw you disappear," she said "Then it felt like I was falling. The next thing I knew, Thad and I were sitting on the ground in a field of really tall grass, and it was raining. We were both shook up from all the monsters. He tried to explain things to me, but I was kind of hysterical for a while there. It took us a couple of hours of walking around before Thad figured out where we were. I'm glad he has a good sense of direction, or I'd probably still be stuck there."

We stared at each other, and I motioned for her to continue.

"Oh...um...we found this road—really just a path—and we followed it until we came to this farm in the middle of nowhere. Thad told me to hide in one of the barns because of how I was dressed. He was gone a while, and I fell asleep. When he came back, he had this dress and told me to put it on. We spent the night in the barn, and the next day, we went into town."

"Spent the night?"

"It was too late to travel, so yeah. The farmer and his family never knew we were there. We ate some bread Thad had with him, and we went to sleep."

"So what was it, like a hayloft or something?"

"Yeah, there was some hay in there," she replied. "It was nice. It gave us time to talk."

"Talk," I repeated. "So you just talked?"

"Did you know he fought in the Civil War?"

When she mentioned the Civil War, I remembered my interview with the man and —

"My webcam!" I said. "I was interviewing him about his time in the war when you came over. It has been recording this whole time!"

CHAPTER 11

As soon as we got to my house, we both rushed inside to the computer.

"Play it back," Lacy said. "Play the part where we left."

"Well, duh," I said, sitting at the desk. "Unless you'd rather I play the kissy part for you?"

"What kissy part?" She stood up straight with an expression of confusion. For her, Thaddeus had kissed her hand two days ago, so it wasn't fresh in her mind. Then a dawning came and she grinned and got a far-off expression, "That *was* nice. He's a real southern gentleman. You should have seen him in old Kinsville. He was amazing."

I grunted a reply and stopped the machine from recording. Then I hit the play button and it started from the beginning.

"Fast forward," Lacy said.

The frames moved by quickly. The position of the camera took in most of the living room. The left side of the frame caught the window behind the sofa, and on the right side, the T.V. Beyond that, in the middle of the screen, it opened up to the kitchen.

"There!" Lacy said. "He's kissing my hand."

I started it from there. In the video, Lacy stood closest to the camera, near the sofa, partially blocking Thaddeus and me from view. Their bodies became like a sculpted mist. They kept their shape, but the background was visible through them. I rushed in and grabbed Thaddeus' coat. Thaddeus, facing the camera, noticed it was happening and opened his mouth to speak, but we were all gone before the words came. I backed it up a few frames to the point where we were all fading.

"Who do we tell about this?" Lacy asked. "We have video proof that what we say is true."

I shrugged, "I don't know that the video is enough. Videos are faked all the time." I sat there a moment. Then I said, "He told me the doorway to the in-between place he had come through was at the museum, or that's what he thought. He appeared there twice, and the gurelach monster appeared there too."

"Do you think this doorway has moved?"

"To my living room? I don't know. I hope not."

Lacy bent at the waist to examine the image on the monitor more closely.

"What's that there in the window?" she asked, pointing to the left side of the screen. "Is that someone outside or a reflection?"

I leaned in and clicked the button to make the video full screen. It wasn't in focus, and the image was almost washed out from the bright sunlight.

"Yeah," I said and turned toward the window. "Someone was outside in front of the house."

I stood and went to the door. When I stepped out on the porch no one was out there. Lacy stayed with the computer to examine the video.

"They were there the whole time," she called out to me. "They walked up right after I came inside and just hung around out there. Do you think it is one of the neighbors? I can't tell."

"There's no one here now," I replied, but it didn't feel right. I had a feeling I was being watched, and I couldn't help but think that the person who had been outside the window and our disappearance were related.

When it comes to synchronistic events, there are two main camps. On one side, there is the group that says, "Oh, it was just a coincidence." On the other side, there are those that say, "There is no such thing as coincidence." I tend to sit in a less populated third group. While I believe that everything happens for a reason, and that reason is usually the effect of a previous cause, I do think that sometimes something else—perhaps some sort of orchestration—could be at work. I do not necessarily buy into the idea of fate. Coincidences do happen, and even though I might not be able to see their importance at the time, I would never trivialize them as being *just* a coincidence.

"So what now?" Lacy said from the living room.

I went back inside. "I don't know," I replied. "This is huge. The part about the other worlds is huge all by itself. I'm having trouble processing all of this. I'm not sure how to proceed without getting more information from Thaddeus." Lacy was so disheveled and tired. "It sounds silly to say it, but aren't they expecting you back at the hospital?"

She looked at the clock and frowned, "How could I finish my shift after all of this? I've been gone for two days on my lunch hour! Anyway, look at me, I'm a mess."

"Do you want to get a shower or something? I can loan you some clothes."

She rubbed her eyes. "No. Yeah. I mean I think I need to go home."

"What are your parents going to say when you come home in that dress?"

"I'd much rather hear what they say about that than if I came home wearing your clothes."

"Oh," I said.

"Anyway, they're both still at work. I'll call in to the hospital—tell them I'm not feeling well. I need to decompress.

Thad is still out there and...." Her voice halted. She stood. "Call me if anything happens. Just call me no matter what. I have some other things to tell you, but later. I need to rest." Then she patted my cheek, lifted her skirt off the floor so she could walk without stepping on it, and left without another word.

After she left, I pushed the play button to restart the video. While the interview portion was on, I got up to make myself a snack. When I returned a few minutes later, balancing a sandwich on top of my soda can, I was startled by the scene on the monitor.

In the video, there was a woman standing in my house. She was pretty and fit, in her early to mid 30's, and her long, dishwater blonde hair was up. She wore a dark business suit with a knee-length skirt and heels. She held a black satchel.

"What is this?" I whispered.

I immediately felt a shiver knowing a stranger had been in my house. I sat my snack on the desk and plopped myself into the desk chair. The video showed her in my living room. She moved to the kitchen. Salome rubbed against her legs, and the woman bent at the knees (keeping perfect posture!) and scratched Sal's head.

"Traitor," I said to Salome who was trying to nap on the couch. "You're supposed to watch this place while we're gone!"

I turned back to the video. The woman went to the back of the house. She was searching for something. Then it hit me—
What if she's still here!?

I spun around in the chair, stopped, held my breath, listened, breathed....

"Hello?"

No one answered. Why would they?

"Hello?" I tried again, louder. I finally decided to stop being a big chicken, and just go check. There were a lot worse

63

things than finding a good-looking, nicely-dressed woman hiding in my bedroom closet. After a thorough search of the house, and being convinced she was gone, I returned to the computer desk.

I scrolled the video in reverse. She came in through the front door a couple of minutes after I had left. Then I watched it forward at 4x speed. She went through my house, petted my cat, and left the way she came. Was it possible she was there investigating Carl's death? Did the police have questions about me, but were not letting on? Did they secretly send a detective to search my house? Was that even legal?

I watched the video several times, hoping I would catch something I had missed before. Occasionally, I would look over my shoulder to make sure no one or no *thing* had materialized into the room behind me. At some point, Salome crawled into my lap.

I wasn't sure what to do next. I could go back to the library and do more digging, or I could phone the detective and ask if it was okay for me to return to the museum, but I was hesitant to leave the house in case Soosen returned there. Ultimately, I decided to wait. I figured I could get on the web and check the accuracy of Soosen's war story. I suspected if the facts didn't jibe, it would be the internet that was wrong.

No matter how much I wanted to help my dad, I couldn't get my head into the articles about General Burnside and the Battle of Mossy Creek; I was too distracted.

Around 6:30 that evening, I got a call from Lacy.

"It happened again," she said with a shaky voice. "A friend from the hospital called to check on me and told me about it. They're talking about it all over the hospital. Are you okay?"

"I'm fine. What's the matter?"

"A man was brought in to the E.R. about an hour ago. He'd been chewed up. Something tried to eat him, Rob!"

CHAPTER 12

"He died on the table," Lacy said. "My friend said she heard someone from the E.R. say it was bite marks from something big. This is bad. Should I tell someone what we know?"

"They'd never believe you," I said. "Where did it happen? Did they mention where the attack happened?"

"No...I don't know. One of those things is loose in town, isn't it? We have to tell the police so they can be prepared."

"I told you, they won't believe it," I said. "There's something else...." I told her about the woman in my house.

"The police wouldn't send someone there without a warrant," she said. "Could it be a private investigator? Maybe hired by Carl's family?"

"Surely not. He hasn't even been dead for 24 hours yet."

"I don't like this," she said. "Maybe I should tell my parents."

"Do you want to come over tonight and wait for Thaddeus?" I asked. There was silence on her end, and I quickly jumped in again. "If he returns, there's a chance he'll reappear here. He'll know how to fight this thing."

Still, she didn't speak.

"You still there?" I asked.

"I don't know," Lacy said. "It's just that…well…my dad doesn't like me spending so much time over there with your dad out-of-town. Mrs. Kaler who lives next door to you goes to my church, and she called my mom and—"

"This is extenuating circumstances!" I said in a huff. "Besides, this is the twenty-first century. You're eighteen years old. You're a grown woman. You might not have *spent the night* before, but you're here all the time. All. The. Time. What do they say about that?"

"Plenty," she replied. "They say plenty."

"Does it bother you?"

"A little."

I didn't expect it to, but her answer felt like somebody punched me in the stomach. I tried to say something intelligent, but all I could manage was, "Yeah, well…."

"Rob…," she started then paused. "I do want to stay there and wait for Thad, but I just don't need any extra gossip from that blabbermouth Betty Kaler. Even though it's innocent, if she sees my car parked at your place so late, she'll call my mom, and I'll never hear the end of it."

"Sure," I said. "Whatever."

"Don't be mad. Come by and pick me up at eight. I'll tell my folks we're going out to eat and to see a late movie."

"Like a date?"

"It won't be a date, but that's what I'll tell them. That way, Betty Kaler won't see my car parked at your house. I'll see you at eight." She hung up.

"That was Lacy," I said to Sal as I put the phone on the desk. "Apparently, she's bothered that people think she and I might be a couple. *Bothered.* She stayed a whole night in a hay loft with the time traveler like a character in a romance novel, but with me she's afraid of what people will think."

Sal licked herself and didn't care.

I arrived in front of Lacy's house just before 8 o'clock. Ordinarily, I would have gone up to the door and knocked, but instead, I gave her a call. When she answered, I said, "I'm here." Then I hung up before she could reply.

Less than a minute later, she came down the steps in a brisk walk carrying a large purse, passed through my headlight beams, and opened the passenger door. She tossed the bag into the back seat and climbed in front. She had showered and changed.

"You're upset," she said without looking at me. "I could tell by how you sounded on the phone. Considering what I went through, you should lighten up."

"I'm not upset," I said as I backed out of the driveway. "It's just that people might talk is all. I wouldn't want people to get the wrong idea about us."

She made an exasperated sound and shook her head, "Don't be such a baby."

"Why should you care what they think?" I mumbled. "You could do a lot worse than me." But she either didn't hear me or ignored me.

We drove in silence for a couple of minutes then Lacy said, "I brought my gun."

I was surprised. "Where? In your purse? A handgun? I didn't know you owned a gun."

"I do. It used to belong to my granddad."

"Why didn't you ever mention it?"

She shrugged, "It never came up. I don't tell you everything, you know. We're going to need it. If those monsters come through, I don't want to be helpless."

"Thaddeus kept talking about that weapon he dropped when he first popped in...."

"We should go to the museum and find it," Lacy said. "You never did a proper search. You said so yourself."

67

"The police have been there this whole time," I responded with a tone of resignation. "If it was there, I'm sure they found it."

"So? From the description, it doesn't really look like a weapon, right? They probably thought it was part of an exhibit and left it."

"Could be," I said.

"It won't hurt to swing by there," she said. "Maybe we can get in."

We arrived at the museum a few minutes later. The front of the building was illuminated by the security lights in the small parking lot, and the police barricade tape was still stretched across the railing and door. I did not pull in.

"Oh well," I said.

"Park in the back," Lacy said. "We'll go in there."

"If it's taped in the front, it'll be taped in the back," I said.

"We can get past tape," she said. "I was thinking it would be easier to hide the car back there next to that hedge."

"I'm not going to hide the car!" I said. "What if the police come back? What if we contaminate their investigation?"

"It's your dad's place of business, isn't it? What are they going to do, arrest you? They've had all last night and all day today to dust for prints or whatever they do. Anyway, they think it was an animal attack, for crying out loud. We won't contaminate a thing."

"Then why are we hiding? Why not just park in the front?"

"Jeez, Rob, just pull around back and park. I'll go in and look by myself if you're too chicken."

"Don't start with your chicken argument, I—"

"Bok."

"Lacy—"

"Bok bok."

"Shut up. Fine. I'll pull around."

I took the next street, circled around, and pulled in the entrance to the back lot. There was a nice shadowy spot between the building and the hedge.

"Got a flashlight?" Lacy asked after I'd shut off the engine and headlights.

I pressed a button on my key chain and a single, LED bulb flickered.

"Awesome," Lacy said, her voice thick with sarcasm. "Is that all you've got?"

"There might be one in the trunk," I said. "I don't remember."

There was a flashlight in the trunk, but the best it could give us was a dim yellow ring of light.

"It'll have to do," Lacy said, as she retrieved the snub-nosed revolver from her bag.

"Do you have a permit for it?" I asked nodding at the gun.

"Nope. It was passed on to me after my granddad died. No paperwork. My dad says it's better that way."

"Have you ever used it?" I asked.

"I shot it some a few years ago. My dad showed me how to load it and clean it."

I was dubious. "Maybe you should leave it in the car. If the police—"

"You should be more afraid of the monsters than the police," she said as she pushed the gun into her waistband. "There were hundreds of those things. Hundreds!"

"If the cops find us here—"

"Bok bok," she called over her shoulder as she ducked under the police tape. "Get over here and unlock the door before someone sees us."

I sighed and followed her to the back door of the museum.

"This is a side of you I haven't seen," I said as I slid my key into the deadbolt lock. "I don't think I'm comfortable with it."

"Good. You've been a little too comfortable with me for a little too long."

69

There was some light coming from the exit signs, but just enough to find the doors in an emergency, not really enough to do any serious searching. It was cooler inside than I usually keep it.

"It's like a refrigerator in here," I said. "The cops cranked up the A.C. Dad never lets me turn it down this cool. Let me go adjust the thermostat, and we'll look around for that astra weapon."

"Where did Thad come in the first time?" she asked. "We can start there."

"Over there," I pointed with my tiny flashlight. "Between the gift shop and the display cases for the Civil War. He was stuck in the floor. Maybe that's where the weapon is—buried in the concrete there."

I went into the other side of the main gallery to turn off the air conditioning while Lacy investigated the spot where Thaddeus made his grand entrance.

"The glass is broken on this display case," Lacy said.

"Yeah, I know. That's the case Carl told me about before he...well, you know."

I made my way back to Lacy through the dark gallery using my little LED key chain to light the way. Lacy shined the other flashlight around.

"Does anything look out of place or different?" she asked.

"Not really," I said. "But it is difficult to tell in the dark."

"By the way," she said, "I forgot to mention it, but the museum can have that dress if you want. It's torn and needs to be cleaned, but I'm sure period clothing like that is rare."

"Yeah, that would be great."

We walked around together, trying to be thorough. We checked beneath tables and racks, and we examined all of the cases and exhibits. We avoided it in the beginning, but eventually, we wound up near the spot where Carl had been killed. There was still a dark stain on the floor and several of the little numbered markers the detectives had left.

"Let's not get any closer," I said.

Lacy nodded and moved to the next room. She directed her beam to the walls in the gift shop. "What's that up there?"

High up, near the ceiling, something protruded from the brick wall. It reminded me of a large, curved beak.

"Whoa," I gasped. "That looks like gold. That's got to be it, but half of it is embedded in the bricks. How'd it get up there?"

"Do you have a ladder?"

"Not one that tall here," I said. "There's an extension ladder in the shed at home. We'll have to come back."

"And we'll have to smash the bricks to get it out," she said.

I frowned at the thought of what the local Historical Society and the museum board would say after I knocked a hole in the original brickwork of that old building, but I agreed.

"Come on," I said. "Being here makes me nervous."

Then both of us were startled by a commotion outside. There was a yowl and the clattering of metal. We held our breath and listened.

"What do you think?" I said. "Cops?"

"Cats."

There was a heavy thump against the back door.

"That's no cat," I said.

CHAPTER 13

We stood at the threshold where the main gallery joined the gift shop and stared across the large room at the windowless back door. There was another thump, but it was softer. Lacy pulled her gun. There were a few seconds of silence. A shuffling and scratching came from the front of the building on the plywood where Carl had boarded up the windows.

"Rob?" Lacy whimpered.

"Hold on," I said. I slipped through the shelves and racks of the gift shop and peered through the window of the front door. Outside, the yellow and black police tape swayed in a gentle breeze. The parking lot was empty. Farther out on the street, cars drove past, the drivers oblivious.

"What do you see?" Lacy asked.

"Nothing. There's nothing—wait..."

A shadow fell briefly over the lot. Something had passed in front of one of the security lights and close enough to the source to block out most of the light. I had to press the side of my face to the window to see it. There was a small naked man-thing up there hanging off the side of the light pole like a koala.

72

The creature didn't notice me; it was too interested in the cars driving on the street below it.

"There's one of the monsters out front on the light pole," I said. "We should head out the back now while we have a chance." I turned to Lacy, but she was already on her way to the back door. By the time I got outside, Lacy had her phone to her ear.

"Who are you calling?"

"The police," she said. "They need to see this thing."

"Well, keep going and make the call in the car," I said as I shut the museum door behind me. I didn't waste time locking it. I jogged over and joined Lacy, and we got into the car at the same time.

"Yes," she said, "I'm calling to report something on a light pole in front of the museum."

I cranked the car and backed out of our hiding place. "It's on Fifth Street," I said. "Tell them Fifth Street."

"Fifth Street," she said. "It looks like a naked man, but it's not. You should be ready to shoot it....no just come see for yourself. Please, just send a car over. Tell the officers to be careful...no...no...it's not a man, it just looks like a man....no!" Lacy stopped talking and pressed the button to end the call.

"Didn't believe you?" I said.

"No, but that's okay. They'll send a car anyway. In a town this small, there's not much else for them to do. I just hope they listened to my warning. They have no idea what they're up against." When I got to the street, she said, "Pull around, so we can keep an eye on the thing until they get here."

I took a left and passed the museum, crossed the intersection, and parked in a corner lot on the other side of 5th Street. We had a clear view of the creature. It had crawled up to the very top of the pole and was perched up there like a gargoyle. Electrical lines, stacked four high and running in five directions were above and below the creature's position. We sat

73

and watched it for a couple of minutes, and the thing didn't move.

"I wonder what it's doing," I said.

"Nothing good," she replied. "Look, here they come."

The police cruiser approached from the opposite direction and crept past the museum with a spotlight on the building then pulled into the front lot and parked askew. We continued to wait across the street. The two officers sat in the car a moment while one of them talked on the radio. The two men got out and peered around.

"Up, you morons," Lacy mumbled from the seat beside me. "Look up."

They didn't look up.

"I told the dispatcher it was on the light pole," she said shaking her head. "Just look up. This is ridiculous!" She opened her door, climbed out, and yelled across the street. "It's up there, guys! On top of the pole!"

The officers spun around. Lacy stabbed a finger toward the sky, "Up!"

One of the men finally saw the gurelach. He took a step back and tapped his partner on the arm. Both men gaped up at the naked creature.

"Sir?" one of them called out with a chuckle, "Sir, how did you get up there?"

"It's not a man!" Lacy yelled. "It's dangerous!"

"We'll handle this!" one of them yelled back.

His partner spoke into his shoulder mike then waved up at the gurelach.

"Sir, we've called the fire department! They'll be here with a ladder! You sit tight!"

"No!" Lacy yelled.

Meanwhile, the traffic on 5th Street continued its intermittent flow, although a few of the motorists did tap their brakes when they passed the cruiser.

The monster stirred and stood erect.

"Sir, please be still!" one the cops yelled. "We're going to get you down!"

"Shoot it!" Lacy demanded. "Shoot it now!"

"Ma'am, you need to get back in your car!"

"We should have shot it ourselves," she said to me.

Impulsively, Lacy headed off on foot toward the street. Her right arm was crooked up behind her back to conceal the gun in her hand.

"Lacy!" I opened my door and got out. "No!"

One of the cops held up a hand, "Ma'am, go back to your vehicle!"

Lacy kept walking, eyes on the monster. The fire engine siren wailed a couple of blocks over.

"Ma'am stop right there!"

When she made it to the sidewalk on our side of the street, she must have thought she was close enough, because she let her hand drop.

"Gun!" the cop warned his partner as he reached for his service pistol.

The traffic on 5th Street prevented the officer from pointing or firing at her. He stepped to the edge of the street with his hand in the air in an attempt to stop the cars. Lacy ignored him anyway and brought the revolver up.

The gurelach must have sensed her intent, because that's when it made its move. The thing leapt out, grabbed one of the thick power lines with a clawed hand, and used the momentum to launch itself out over the street like an acrobat on a trapeze.

Lacy's gun fired, but she didn't mean for it to. The creature slammed down onto the trunk of a passing car then to the pavement and rolled. Tires screeched. Then the thing was loping like an ape down the centerline, away from us toward Broadway. Lacy missed it.

The cops were torn between pursuing the naked acrobat and arresting Lacy for discharging a weapon within the city limits.

"Get back in the car!" I yelled to Lacy before they could make up their mind.

She was noticeably frustrated that the thing had gotten away. She was caught up in the moment, and had not considered the amount of trouble she'd be in if the police crossed the street after her.

The siren screamed, and the red lights of the fire truck played on the buildings and street ahead of its arrival.

"Now, Lacy!"

With reluctance, she obeyed. The fire truck rounded the corner and pulled to a stop in the road between us and the police. As soon as Lacy was in the car, I backed out of there and gunned it away from the commotion down a side street.

If the cops had gotten a good look at my car, I figured I could expect a visit from Detective Barnes about why a vehicle matching the description of mine was fleeing the scene of an incident involving gunfire and a naked man. I hoped the two officers had been too distracted by everything else to get an accurate description of my car. It was night, and I was certain I had been too far away for them to get my license plate number.

"Let's hope they aren't able to identify us," I said. "It was one thing to call the cops; another thing altogether to shoot at the thing with them around. That was just dumb."

"Don't you talk to me like that, Rob! They weren't doing anything about it. That thing could have killed somebody and still might."

"They could arrest you! Then what?"

Her only response was to shake her head.

"We know where the weapon is," I said. "We should focus on getting that. We'll go back to my house and get the ladder."

"We should go ahead and call your house. Maybe Thad came through while we were away."

"I don't know if he'd know what to do if he heard a phone ring, but...okay."

CHAPTER 14

The answering machine picked up when Lacy dialed my home line, which was no surprise. She called out to him on the phone, but if Thaddeus had been there in my house, I'm sure Lacy's disembodied voice only confused and frightened him.

We arrived there a few minutes later and went inside. He wasn't there.

"Are you hungry?" I asked and went into the kitchen. "Do you want a sandwich before we go back out?"

"I'm too wound up to eat," she said. "What time is it?"

"Almost ten," I said as I opened the fridge. "I'm having a sandwich. I haven't eaten since that late lunch."

"Okay," she said with an impatient sigh. "Fix one for me too."

"What time are your parents expecting you back?"

"I told them it would be around midnight." She sat at the kitchen table.

"That should be plenty of time to get that weapon. I hope rye bread is okay. That's all we have."

She nodded about the food and said. "I think there is more at the museum than just the weapon."

"Like what?"

78

"When I was in 1877, Thad told me about these doorways to other worlds. He said sometimes they open naturally by themselves, and sometimes they open because there is a *key* to open them. He said the natural openings are random. The fact that he keeps coming here to this time must be because of one of those keys. It has to be. He and the monster and me—we all appeared at the museum. That's not random. The door to this other world must be at the museum, and the key must be there. It has to be somewhere in all that old stuff."

"There aren't any old keys at the museum," I said and slid a plate over to her.

"It might not look like a key that we know. It could be anything."

"I don't know what it would be," I said. "I don't remember anything at the museum that is odd or unknown. Dad never mentioned anything. All of the artifacts there are properly identified—nothing otherworldly. Maybe this 'key' is in 1877. Maybe there is no key in this time."

"Maybe it exists in both times?" Lacy suggested.

It did sound logical. "Sort of like an anchor between the two points?" Then I shook my head. "That doesn't explain why we slipped through here in my house. The time was the same but not the location, not if the key is somewhere in or around the museum. Anyway, if a key has been there all these years, why is it just now opening the doorway?"

"I don't know," she shrugged and took a bite of her sandwich. "Maybe the storm triggered it."

After we ate, we went outside and got the ladder. Lacy helped me lift it to the luggage rack on top of the car. Once it was strapped in place with bungee cords, we headed back to the museum. Unfortunately, we wouldn't be getting in there again until much later.

The patrol car was still parked in front of the museum, and it had been joined by a second. There was a TV news crew there too. The astra would have to wait.

"Might as well take me home," Lacy said. "We can try again tomorrow."

I crossed over 5th Street and drove right past. When I got to 7th Street, another police car, blue lights flashing, blew through the intersection headed south.

"I wonder what that's about," Lacy said.

"Probably on a different call."

I took a right there and headed south myself, not to follow it, but because it was on our way to Lacy's house. The cruiser sailed through the stoplight at the next intersection. Other motorists parted to give it room. Then it came to a stop so suddenly, it almost set its nose on the pavement. There in the glow of streetlights, headlights, and the flashing blue was the hunched form of the gurelach.

"There it is," Lacy whispered.

The doors opened on the police car, but before the officers could get out, the monster was on the move again. It bounded up on their hood, then over the cruiser's light bar. There was a pedestrian on the sidewalk in front of the drug store. The gurelach noticed him.

"Oh no," I said.

It pounced. Lacy cried out in surprise. The man raised his arm in a defensive move, but it did no good. They tumbled to the ground. The gurelach's jaw unhinged, its wide mouth got wider, and its saw-blade teeth sank into the man's torso. Chilling screams reached me even at that distance with my windows rolled up. The creature braced itself on the sidewalk for leverage then, with a yank of its head, ripped out part of the man's ribcage. Everywhere more screams erupted from horrified onlookers. The gurelach grinned over its shoulder. Gore dripped from the curved, splintered rib bones and shreds of human flesh in its teeth. The police rushed toward the attacker, guns drawn.

"Go! Go! We have to go!" Lacy cried.

I mashed the accelerator and cut the car to the left, swerving momentarily into the oncoming lane. I was met with flashing lights and horns. I swerved back. My vision blurred from my own tears.

Lacy's house was well away from the commotion. I parked on the street, and we sat in the car for a few minutes so she could compose herself before facing her parents.

"What are we going to do, Rob?" she said through sniffles. "Are more of those things going to come through? What if Thad doesn't come back to help us?"

"I don't know," I said, replying to all three questions.

"The police should believe it now that they have seen it. I just hope there is something they can do about it."

"Can you imagine what would happen if all the creatures we saw this morning came through here in Kinsville? It would be the end of everything."

We were quiet for a moment, and she opened her door. "I'm going in. I doubt I'll sleep tonight. Maybe I'll get on the internet and see if I can find a way to make this stop. If Thad doesn't come back, we're on our own."

I got out and went around the car.

"You don't have to walk me to the house," she said as she reached back into the car for her purse.

"I want to."

She was about to cry again. She made a move to hug me then hesitated. I pulled her in and held her.

"You're a good friend," she said and buried her face in my chest.

"You're my *best* friend." I whispered. I can't remember ever wanting to kiss her more than I did right then, but I didn't do it.

CHAPTER 15

I stayed up until almost 3 A.M. in my living room, but Thaddeus Soosen did not return. I eventually fell asleep where I sat with Salome in my lap. Just after 7 A.M., there was a knock on my door.

"Huh?" I said, still partially asleep.

The knocking was loud and persistent. I rubbed my eyes, and pushed myself up off the couch. "Okay! I'm coming!"

When I opened the door, I found Detective Barnes and a uniformed police officer on my front porch.

I felt a rush of panic, but I spoke calmly. "Yes?"

"Good morning, Mr. Bright. May we come in?"

"Uh…I just woke up."

"We just have a few questions. We won't be long."

"Is there something wrong?" I asked, still standing in the doorway.

"We just have some questions. You could come outside, if you prefer."

"Sorry," I shrugged. "Come on in."

I stood aside so they could enter. The two men came in, but they stayed near the door.

"I can make some coffee. Would you like some coffee?" I said, unable to control the nervousness in my voice.

"Thank you," Barnes said. "But we're fine."

I motioned to the couch. "Please sit."

The detective accepted the invitation, but the other man continued to stand. Barnes pulled a notebook from the inside pocket of his navy blazer. "Thank you, Robert. We don't want to intrude too long. I was just hoping you could help us out."

"Sure," I said, taking a seat in my computer chair. "Anything."

"Do you know about the attacks in town?"

"Attacks?" I feigned ignorance, but I didn't think I was convincing. "No."

Barnes stared at me a moment, reading my face. "There were more attacks yesterday like what happened at the museum and two more people were killed."

"That's horrible," I said. "Do you think the attacks are related?"

"It's likely," he nodded. "This might sound like a crazy question, but do you and your dad happen to own a chimpanzee or know anyone who does?"

It took me off-guard. "No," I said. "How would I get a chimpanzee? Where would I keep it?"

"I had to ask," Barnes said. "The description given by witnesses sounds a lot like a chimp."

"That's....that's—" I didn't know what to say.

"Crazy. Yeah, I know. Anyway, witnesses reported the ape or man or whatever in the street in front of the museum last night—*your* museum. That's quite a coincidence." The detective waited for me to say something. When I didn't, he went on. "And we even received an anonymous call at the station last night telling us about it and telling us to shoot it. Would you know anything about any of that?"

"No," I said. He didn't believe me.

"The call was made from a cell phone. We're still trying to track the person down so we could question them, but...." He stopped talking and shrugged. "Well, Robert, I'm sorry to have disturbed you so early. You don't seem to be harboring any chimps here. I did want to let you know too that we're finished inside the museum. You can get back in there now. I know you have work to do. Tell your dad that the insurance adjuster stopped by yesterday. I told her she could come back today. I hope that was okay."

"Yeah. Absolutely." I said.

He stood and started to leave then turned back. "By the way, how did things go with your reenactor friend?"

"It went well," I said after a brief pause. "Our project is coming together."

"Glad to hear it," he smiled. "What sort of project is it? I'm kind of a history buff."

"Civil War," I said. "It's about a veteran of the Civil War."

"Is he still in town?"

"No," I said. "He had to get back."

He continued to read my face like he didn't trust me. Finally he said, "Have a good day."

I said goodbye then Salome and I watched the two men through the window until their car pulled out of the driveway.

"That was weird," I told Sal.

Over a bowl of cornflakes, I watched the morning news report on the gurelach attack in downtown Kinsville. Despite the numerous eyewitness accounts of a monster, the news anchors referred to the beast as an animal, and speculated it might be an ape, possibly an escaped pet chimpanzee. They even cited a pet chimpanzee attacking a human in California years before. They kept showing a blurry video, shot from a jostled phone, of the gurelach running down the street in Kinsville. The way the creature moved brought credibility to the pet ape theory.

My phone rang. It was Lacy. As soon as I picked up, she said, "This chimpanzee story is ridiculous! Who in Kinsville would own a chimp? And they have yet to explain why the thing was hairless!"

"The video was so bad you couldn't tell it was hairless," I said.

"But those cops saw it!" she said. "They know! Those people on the street saw it too!"

"They came to see me a few minutes ago," I said. "They wanted to know if I owned a chimpanzee."

"The police? Are you serious?! They were there! They saw it!"

"I know."

"You aren't in trouble are you? Did they ask about the gun? Did they ask about me?"

"No," I replied. "I don't think they have put the two together, but I do think they are suspicious. The detective acted like he didn't trust me."

"We have to go to the museum. We have to get that weapon out of the wall, and we have to go through all those antiques until we find that key. Either we kill these creatures, or we shut off their way into our world. We have to do something."

Without Thaddeus there to instruct us, I doubted we'd be very successful with either of those things, but I agreed with Lacy. People were dying; we had to try.

"Good morning, by the way," I said.

"What's so good about it?"

"Right. Meet you there in an hour."

CHAPTER 16

The ladder was still on my car when I drove to the museum. Lacy was there waiting for me. Even though we were officially cleared to be in the building, we still parked in the back lot. I didn't want someone to see my vehicle, and take it as an invitation to come inside.

"Do you have a hammer to break up the brick?" Lacy asked as we unloaded the ladder and carried it to the back door.

"Let's see if we can pull the astra out without breaking anything," I replied. "I'd rather not catch any grief from the museum board, and I sure don't want to give Edith Haber any ammunition against my dad or the museum."

"The windows were broken and a man was killed in here yesterday. How will Edith react to that?"

"I don't know," I said. "But that was beyond our control. I do have some control over smashing bricks."

"But we're extracting a magical weapon—probably priceless—that belongs to a time traveler so we can kill a monster from another world."

"Yeah, I think there is a clause in the museum bylaws about that," I replied trying to be facetious. "How about I just try to pull it out first?"

"Like Arthur and Excalibur...."

"If I can't do it the gentle way, we'll use the hammer."

We took the ladder into the gift shop, stood it beneath the astra, extended it up to its full height and leaned it against the wall. The top of the ladder rested about two feet below the weapon.

"Steady the ladder for me," I said. "I'm going up."

I kept my eyes on the golden object as I climbed.

"Don't look down," Lacy said.

I got three rungs from the top and stopped. I heard the back door open.

"I thought we locked the door," I said.

"So did I," Lacy replied.

Our view of the back door was blocked by a wall that divided the gift shop from the main gallery. We waited, motionless, for whoever had entered the building to come around the corner. When a reasonable amount of time had passed, I said, "Hello? Who's there?"

"Oh, hello?" said a woman's voice. Her heels clicked on the floor as she moved through the gallery. When she came around, I recognized her as the woman from the video in my house. She was dressed exactly the same and carried the same satchel. She was even prettier in person. I tried to pretend as though I'd never seen her before.

"Can we help you?" I asked.

"I didn't realize anyone was here," she said. She smiled at Lacy then up at me. There was a brief, but noticeable, widening of her eyes when she saw the astra. She quickly masked her interest in the object and extended her hand to Lacy. "Hi, I'm Mary with South Valley Property and Casualty. I'm the claims adjuster."

I didn't believe her. An insurance adjuster for the museum would have had no reason to go to my house. Furthermore, there was the whole breaking-and-entering thing.

Lacy shook her hand. "I'm just holding the ladder," she replied with a friendly chuckle. "Rob is the one you should talk with."

The woman smiled up at me, "Rob I presume? Are you in charge here?"

I decided to play along. I climbed down the ladder, "I'm Robert. My dad is the director here, but he left me in charge while he is away. The police said you were here yesterday. Did you get a chance to look at the damage?"

"Not really. They shooed me away," she replied and shook my hand. She stole a glance at the astra. "Is your dad around?"

"No," I said. "But I can show you the damage. If you have any questions you can always give him a call. The windows caught the worst of it. There's also some damage to the roof."

Her eyes searched the place as I spoke, but she didn't open her satchel or write anything down, "And that display case over there?"

I followed her gaze over to the small gallery next to the gift shop and to the case that had been damaged by the gurelach.

"Yeah," I said, "that too, I suppose."

"Were any of the historical items damaged? Are any missing?"

I shook my head, "I don't think so, but to be honest, I'm just getting in here myself. I'm sure dad will do a thorough inventory when he gets back from his trip."

"When he does that inventory, please tell him to report any missing items. I'll give you an E-mail address for that," she said and walked over to the display. She kneeled in front of the broken case and studied the items inside.

Meanwhile, Lacy mouthed something to me I didn't catch then moved to take down the ladder.

Mary was right next to the stain on the floor.

"That's where Carl died," I said. "He did maintenance work for us here." I pointed to the floor near her feet.

She looked at the blood stain and stood. "I saw that on the news. That was sad. The news reports say it was an escaped monkey or something. Bizarre."

She returned to me, took another quick peek at the astra when she thought I wasn't looking, and said in a business-like manner, "What I would like first is a list of all the items on display and any additional items you might have in storage. We'll need a list for our records for comparison."

"We sent an updated inventory list to South Valley last August after everything in the permanent collection was reappraised. I remember helping dad catalog everything."

"Did you? I didn't know," she said with a distracted tone as she watched Lacy move the ladder. "Perhaps it is on file at the office."

I was starting to get annoyed. "Look, my main concern is the damage to the building. This all needs to be repaired so we can reopen the museum. Shouldn't you be writing stuff down or something?"

Then there was a loud noise from the main gallery. The three of us stared at the entrance to the room then at each other.

"Is someone else here?" the woman asked.

"Excuse me," I said. "I'll be right back."

I went into the gallery and found Thaddeus Soosen sprawled in the floor next to an overturned pedestal. He was soaked, muddy, and out-of-breath.

"You're back," I said. "Am I glad to see you! Are you hurt?"

He sat up and put on his wet hat. Water dripped from the end of his nose. With a sorrowful voice he said, "I have lost Miss Lacy."

"No," I said. "She's here. She's fine."

He jumped to his feet. "Where?" Then he pushed past me into the gift shop.

"No, wait," I tried to prevent him, but it was too late. I followed him right out.

89

He stopped dead next to the counter by the gift shop's cash register. "Maribeth," he said with obvious surprise.

A sly grin formed on the woman's lips. "Hello, Thaddeus. It's been a very long time."

There was a heavy pause then they both went for their guns.

CHAPTER 17

I was in the middle of an armed standoff. I never saw the woman draw her little semi-automatic pistol; it just sort of appeared in her hand.

"Hey!" Lacy squawked and took a step back against a postcard rack. She fumbled around behind her back and came out with her own gun.

"Whoa!" I yelled. "Lacy, no! Thaddeus, what's this about?"

"Drop it, lady!" Lacy yelled, taking a wide stance and using both hands to hold her gun.

The woman was unperturbed. She never took her eyes off Thaddeus. "I'm here for the box. Where is it?"

"Ain't got it," he replied. "It ain't here."

"It's here," she said. "If it wasn't here, *you* wouldn't be here. You've been careless and let the gurelachs through."

"You know about the gurelachs?" I asked. "Who are you?"

"Stop pointing your gun at him!" Lacy demanded.

The woman cut her eyes over at Lacy then back to Soosen. "You didn't waste any time finding some female companionship, did you, Thaddeus? She's a bit young."

"Lacy ain't no saloon girl, if that's what you're sayin'."

"'Lacy' certainly sounds like a saloon girl name," the woman smirked.

"Saloon girl?" Lacy said. "What?"

"I remember you were sweet on that one other whore — the one in San Francisco — "

"Whore!?" Lacy spat.

"What was her name again? Calico? Crinoline?"

"Petticoat Prudy," Thaddeus said. "That was her playactin' name at the burly-q. 'Tweren't her real name."

"I should hope not."

"Everybody put your guns away!" I interjected. "Let's just talk about this."

"You look different, Maribeth," Thaddeus said. "You look a bit older. You sound different too."

"Yeah, I'm older," she chuckled. "You have no idea."

"And for all your talk about whores and saloon girls, you should take a gander at your own dress. Your legs and ankles show. It is downright shameful and obscene."

"Put the guns away or I'll call the cops," I said.

"If I see you touch a phone, I will execute the saloon girl first," Maribeth said.

"Shut up!" Lacy yelled. "In case you haven't noticed, I have a gun on you right now!"

Finally, Thaddeus slid his revolver back into its holster inside his coat and put his hands up. "Don't call for your coppers, Mr. Bright. She ain't about to kill me. Even if I did have that box, she wouldn't shoot me until she got it."

"I could shoot you without actually killing you, you idiot. I can make it hurt. I can make you tell me where it is," Maribeth said, continuing to aim her pistol at Thaddeus.

"What box?!" Lacy said. "What is going on?! Who is this woman?"

"She's not from the insurance company," I said.

"Well, duh!"

"She's the woman my webcam recorded," I said.

Maribeth was surprised, yet amused by this news.

"She's the one who broke into your house? Why didn't you say anything?"

"She must be another time traveler," I said, mostly to myself. I pointed up to the gold crescent in the wall. "Does this have something to do with that?"

"You found my astra!" Thaddeus exclaimed.

Maribeth turned and looked up at the weapon then turned back to address Thaddeus. "You are so careless. You lost your astra *and* you told them about it? No wonder Östric is done with you."

"Östric said that?" Thaddeus asked, crestfallen. Then he puffed out his chest. "Well...I was done with him first. You tell him so."

"We'll tell him together," Maribeth said. "Now, inform your *trollop* if she doesn't lower her gun, I will be forced to shoot her."

"Trollop?!" Lacy was shaking either from fear or from rage. "You lower *your* gun. I've got the drop on *you*."

"Do it," Thaddeus said to Lacy.

"But—"

"You ain't no killer, Miss Lacy, but Maribeth is. Killin' is her profession."

With reluctance, and even though it appeared she had the advantage, Lacy obeyed.

"The young man is right, Maribeth. Ain't no reason we can't talk on this. We put our guns down; you do the same. Ain't got to be no shootin'."

She didn't move. "You're dripping a puddle in the floor," she said to Thaddeus.

"It was rainin' where I came from," he replied.

"It was raining *when* you came from," Maribeth corrected. She put her satchel on the floor then knelt and opened it just enough to stick her hand inside. She pulled out a stack of $100 bills bound with a rubber band. She stood again and tossed the money to Lacy.

"What's this?" Lacy said.

"Run down the street to the men's store and buy our boy some dry and modern clothes."

Lacy started to throw the money back, but Maribeth aimed her little pistol at Lacy's face.

"Listen carefully," she said. "Get him a suit. Nothing fancy. Size forty-two long. Classic fit. He'll need socks and underwear too; use your own judgment on the sizes for those. The shoes can wait, but get a belt in case the pants are too big."

"I'm not your servant," Lacy said through gritted teeth.

"You are nothing to me at all," Maribeth said. "Now run along."

Lacy turned to me and Thaddeus. "Aren't you going to do something?"

I cleared my throat to speak, but nothing came to mind.

"I would be grateful for some dry clothes, Miss Lacy," Soosen said.

I just nodded to Lacy to go. She frowned at us and stomped out, mumbling curses under her breath. Just before the door closed behind her, Maribeth said, "Come back alone, and don't forget the receipt."

Maribeth let her gun hand drop to her side once Lacy was gone. Thaddeus had not moved from his spot near the counter, and I followed his lead since he knew—and to some extent feared—this woman. She stared at us in silence then walked closer.

She said, "When agents noticed the news story of this supposed animal attack, Östric sent me to investigate. This little town had a history of gurelach activity, and he suspected there might be a natural gateway here. Then, yesterday morning, whom do I see sitting in front of the museum, but Thaddeus Soosen. We thought the monsters had killed you and Virgil back in the eighteen seventies. We had no idea you'd pop up again. When I saw how you were dressed in those clothes, I knew something wasn't right. Even Östric was surprised by this movement through time."

"I am also surprised," Thaddeus said.

"Your medallion," she said and held out her hand. "Give it to me before you get pulled through again. Östric believes it has linked itself with the box and keeps looping you back and forth through time. We have to sever the link."

"Then if you take it, I cannot go back again."

"You can't go back anyway," she said. "You disappeared then and reappeared in this time. There is no historical record of you after that."

"I've been back to old Kinsville twice already," he said.

"Not permanently."

"That doesn't mean—"

"It means that you can't go back! If you went back and lived out the rest of your life from that time, your presence would disrupt everything. It would change the timeline."

"I don't understand what you say."

Maribeth huffed, "It would alter history. Give me the medallion."

"For me, this history has not yet happened!"

"If you went back, this time we're in now would be different. It could be drastically different."

Thaddeus scoffed, "Am I now so important to affect the history of an entire world?"

"This is different! You moved through time! Everything is important when it comes to time. There is a reason why the Ancients forbade it. The slightest, most insignificant changes in a timeline could start a chain of events that could result in something catastrophic. The past is, and we must leave it be."

"I can't stay here. My momma—"

"Your momma has been dead for more than a century!" She lifted her gun again and pointed it at him. She stepped in, pushed his coat aside and pulled the watch chain on his vest. The chain was not connected to a watch after all. A golden disc was attached. Engraved on it, was a symbol of interlocking circles, and in the center was a small, blue gemstone or crystal. She held it up, and the medallion dangled on the end of its chain like the implement of a hypnotist. After inspecting it, she pushed it into a pocket of her own suit jacket. "This is your own fault," she said "You shouldn't have stolen the box. You were warned about its power."

"Please, Maribeth, I had to serve Östric for ten years to earn my medallion."

Then she motioned at me with the gun. I pointed at myself and said, "Me?"

"You," she said. "Climb up there and get the astra for me."

"Okay." I moved past Thaddeus and went to get the ladder from where Lacy had moved it.

"I can get it," Thaddeus offered.

"I think we've all learned that you can't be trusted with that kind of power anymore. No, the boy can get it."

"What's to stop *me* from using it?" I said as I put the ladder in place. "I could use it against you."

"Astrae are special weapons," she replied. "They will function only for specific people. They are not of this Earth."

"Are *you* of this Earth?" I asked.

"Quite," she said. "Now climb. After you have retrieved it, I want you to get me that inventory list for the museum I asked for earlier."

"I need my astra, Maribeth," Thaddeus said. "My Colt is true, but it don't always put the demons down."

"I'm taking the astra—Östric's orders."

"Why are you bein' like this? We're friends, you and me."

"We were colleagues once, but that was a very long time ago," she said.

"We were more than that," Thaddeus said.

"Where is the box?" She persisted.

"I told you. I ain't got no box. Maybe you should ask Virgil and Emmet where it is."

"Virgil and Emmet are gone," she said. "They disappeared when you did."

Thaddeus was pleased about this and grinned. "Well, I'm sure they will show themselves by the by."

"It took close to one hundred and forty years for you to show up. In all that time, you and the box have been my primary assignment. That's a long time to be frustrated, Thaddeus."

"I am touched that you have pined for me so," he said.

I was just about to reach for the astra, when her words sank in.

"Wait...what?" I said. "Are you saying that you didn't time travel the way he did, but that you actually have been alive and searching for him since eighteen seventy-seven?"

"I have been searching for Thaddeus since eighteen seventy-seven," she said. "I've been alive much longer."

CHAPTER 18

"How old *are* you?" I asked.

"That's a rude question, boy. Can you remove the astra or not?"

The weapon was right above my head. The part that curved out of the bricks was about the size and shape of a banana. It had markings on it—characters from a language I didn't recognize. There was a blue stone on the end of the point.

"It's like it is part of the wall," I said and grabbed it. "It's warm."

"Astrae are always warm," Maribeth said. "See if it will pull free."

I tugged as hard as I could without losing my balance. "No. It's stuck. I guess I'll have to get a hammer after all."

"Come down," she said. "I'll get it myself."

Once I was on the floor again, I took a step back away from the ladder. She motioned with her gun. "Go get that inventory for the museum. I want a complete list."

"What are you hoping to find?" I asked. "Is it that box you're looking for? I've never seen an old box here."

"That's because it ain't here," Thaddeus said.

Maribeth ignored him and grabbed my arm. "What he said earlier about me being a killer is true. Don't try anything while I am on this ladder. I have no problem killing you or anyone you might call to help. Do you understand?"

I nodded.

"Good. Now get away from the ladder, I don't want you looking up my skirt. Go get the museum's inventory catalog and stop asking questions." She glared at me until I went into the office and opened the filing cabinet.

When I came out of the office again with the file, she was on her way up the ladder.

"What is your plan?" I whispered to Thaddeus. "Why did you let her get the upper hand?"

"You were the one who wanted us to put our guns away," he whispered back. "Anyhow, I ain't got no more bullets." Then he leaned in closer. "But it's best she don't know that."

"Where is the box she's looking for?" I asked him. "Do you know?"

"Stop talking!" Maribeth demanded. She took hold of the astra.

"She's going to use the weapon to blast itself out," Thaddeus whispered to me. "You might want to shield yourself."

Maribeth turned her face away from the astra. Suddenly the brick around the golden weapon exploded into tiny bits which sprayed the shop and stung my face. When the dust settled, there was a hole in the wall large enough for a man to crawl through.

"Why'd you do that?!" I said. "I could have done less damage with a hammer!"

Maribeth didn't answer me. She descended the ladder with the astra in her hand. Once she was down, she put the moon-shaped weapon into her satchel.

"Only one more item to collect, and I can finally put all this behind me," she said. She walked over to me and held out her hand. I gave her the file.

"How long has this building been a museum?" she asked as she opened the manila folder.

"Almost forty years. Before that, it was used for storage for about twenty years. Before that, it was a gristmill."

She grunted and leafed through the pages. "Have any of the items ever gone out on loan to other museums?"

"I don't know," I said.

She closed the file and handed it back to me. "Where are the old files? Is there documentation of the contents before your dad's time here?"

"Probably," I replied. "But I wouldn't know where."

She turned back to Thaddeus. "That box must be here in this building. A gurelach attacked a man here, a gurelach was recorded running down the street outside the building last night, and I keep seeing you here. This is where the gateway is. You're being irresponsible in your refusal to tell me. You have sworn to defend against them. Stop lying and tell me where it is!"

"I am not lying! And how am I to kill the demons now that you have taken my astra?"

"I am more concerned about closing off their way through. If you are innocent, then help me. That box holds keys. *The* keys. Do you understand?"

"I figured it out," Thaddeus said. "I figured out what was in it. Emmet had the box, last I saw, on the platform at the Kinsville train station. He and Virgil tried to kill me, Maribeth."

"You stole the box! Of course they tried to kill you."

"No, I believe they wanted it for themselves. They turned you against me."

Maribeth shook her head, "I have trouble believing that. Virgil and Emmet were trusted agents."

"And I am not? I have served the Ancients for almost fifteen years. You only believe Virgil's side because you think me a cad. I tell you, Maribeth, I was not untrue to you."

She sighed, "All right. If you want me to trust you, you're going to have to help me. You cooperate, and I'll put in a good word for you with Östric. So far as everyone knows, you were a traitor. When I phoned Östric yesterday and told him you were alive, he ordered me to kill you once you'd given up the box."

"I am no traitor. I couldn't let those keys get into the wrong hands. I made it so they wouldn't work no more."

An expression of shock washed over Maribeth's face. "What did you do? You opened the box, didn't you? Oh, Thaddeus, what have you done?"

He reached into his pocket and pulled out a short column of white crystal. It was about as long and big around as a man's thumb.

"What is that?" Maribeth asked. The tone of her voice told she already knew and didn't want his confirmation.

"A key, I reckon," Thaddeus replied. "But it is only part of it. It got broke when I was fightin' Virgil for it."

"You fractured one of the keys?" Maribeth was aghast.

He nodded. "A middle one."

She looked faint.

"Are you okay?" I asked.

She cut her eyes at me then back to Thaddeus. "Those keys are ancient—tens of thousands of years old, maybe older. They're priceless not only for who made them but for what they can do."

"They are a danger," Thaddeus said. "Virgil and Emmet wanted the keys either for themselves or for someone else. I took this one out of the box so the set would not be complete. It was in the middle, and I think it was the most important one."

Maribeth reached for the crystal, but Thaddeus closed his hand around it before she could take it.

"I will let you have it in trade," he said. "I want my medallion back...and my astra. If the demons return, I want a means of defense."

"No deal," she said.

"This is a broken piece," he said. "Give me my astra and medallion, and I will give you this piece and tell you where to find the rest of it."

She thought it over. "Just the astra. I keep your medallion until Östric tells me otherwise."

They stared at each other then she pulled the astra out of the bag. They made the trade. Thaddeus put the weapon into his coat.

"Now tell me: where is the rest of this key?" she asked. "Perhaps Östric will know how to repair it."

"It broke into three pieces," he said, "Virgil picked up the other two. The last time I saw him was that night, and he was runnin' back to the train depot. I 'spect he was going to meet up with Emmet. I tried to chase him down, but then I found myself here. One of the demons came here with me, but I killed it."

"That's what happened," I spoke up even though I couldn't really verify the first part of his story.

Maribeth frowned at me. "That doesn't tell me where I can get the rest of the key. You don't know where it is. That doesn't help me at all."

"I told you all I know," he said. "Virgil and Emmet have everything else."

She held up the piece of crystal again to see through it, standing it up between her thumb and index finger. "Do you suppose it still works—this little piece? Do you think this is the cause of your movement through time and not your medallion?"

"Robert here says he saw my medallion take on its blue light. Perchance the medallion and crystal work in concert."

"Maybe, but not exclusively. You keep coming here to this museum," Maribeth said. "I am still inclined to think the other keys are here."

"But I was near the train at first before I came here. Then when I was transported back to Kinsville, I went to a different place away from the depot."

"Was it the mill?" I asked. "This building?"

"No," he said. "I was in a boarding house on the edge of town. It was during the day. I walked back to the train station, but I couldn't find Virgil or Emmet. The train was gone. Then I was here again, and the coppers found me. When me and Miss Lacy got pulled into the in-between and back to my time from Robert's house later on, we ended up outside of town at a little farm. The next day, we walked back to Kinsville. I thought we should look around the mill to see if we could find out what was happening. We hid in the stable outside until nightfall. By then it was rainin' somethin' fierce. I noticed my medallion light up, so I grabbed her hand, but she let go of me, and I lost her. Then I was here again. Ain't no rhyme or reason to how I am poppin' around."

"You took that girl with you?" Maribeth said. "Were you trying to impress her?"

"I got no control over it," he replied.

Maribeth straightened and walked into the small gallery. "I'll have to make a report to Östric," she said. "Before I do, I want to do a thorough inspection of the items in the museum." She motioned to me again. "Boy, come open up these display cases for me."

"My name is not 'boy'. It is Robert or Rob," I said. "And you could be nicer about it."

"Robbie, dear," she said sweetly. "Please open up these display cases or I'll use your face to smash the glass in."

Exasperated, I went into the office for the keys to the cases' locks. When I returned, she and Thaddeus were kneeling in front of the broken case.

"Empty out all the cases," she said to me. "The box might not be here, but perhaps the keys are. Perhaps Emmet or Virgil removed them and hid them with one of the items here."

"So what are we looking for?" I asked. "Are they all white crystals like the one Thaddeus has?"

"I have never seen them," she replied then looked to Thaddeus. "I presume so."

"They are crystals, but they are different colors," Thaddeus said. "Only one of the middle ones was white. Each one is about eight to ten inches long."

"We don't have anything like that here," I said. I knelt next to Maribeth and unlocked the broken case so we could remove the items without cutting ourselves on the shattered glass. "The pieces in this case are all military items of the Civil War and several years prior to eighteen seventy-seven. That piece in front of you is the hardware from a musket. Next to it is a bullet mold. On the lower shelf, a saber belt and two Confederate canteens. No crystals and no box."

"I'll look them over," Maribeth said. "Go open the other cases."

I sighed and moved to the next case. Thaddeus stood and leaned against the wall with his arms crossed. He watched Maribeth remove the items from the broken case.

"You really shouldn't be walkin' about with your legs exposed like that," he said in a low voice. "It is not that I don't appreciate it, but it should be private. At least show some modesty in front of the boy."

"That kid has kept you sheltered, hasn't he?" she said. "The world has changed some since eighteen seventy-seven. Wait until you have a run-in with yoga pants and midriffs...or bikinis."

He took off his hat and fidgeted with it, spinning it around on his fist. Then he ran his fingers through his long, damp hair. He was trying to muster up the courage to say something.

Finally, he said, "You got the wrong notion about me and Miss Lacy. You are still my one and only."

"Shut up, Thaddeus," Maribeth replied without giving him a glance. "Our relationship ended a long time ago—even before you disappeared. I was too old for you back then, and I am much too old for you now."

"It ain't been as long for me as it has for you. I thought we would be able to make amends. Did you forget about me in all that time? Those other girls never meant nothin' to me."

Then the front door opened, and Lacy called out, "Hello? I'm back. Where is everybody? I got the clothes."

"We're in here," I said. "The front gallery."

She came around the corner carrying two large bags. "That's a really big hole in the wall," she said. "Edith Haber is going to be pissed."

CHAPTER 19

Thaddeus took the clothes from Lacy and went into my office to change. Maribeth worked in silence in the front gallery while Lacy and I removed items from glass display cases in the larger main gallery.

"This has gotten out of hand," Lacy whispered to me. "Maybe we should call that detective and just tell him everything."

"Maribeth said she'd kill anyone we called, and I believe her," I whispered back.

Lacy rolled her eyes. "She's all talk."

I handed her a tray of flint arrowheads and points. "Put those over there on that pedestal so they don't get broken. Thaddeus doesn't think she's all talk. There's something else. Earlier, when you were gone, she mentioned that she's really old. She's been around since at least the eighteen hundreds—no time travel. She's literally that old. Can you believe that?"

"I'm ready to believe just about anything."

I passed her a clay bottle. "That is several hundred years old. Please be careful."

She took it to the pedestal and set it next to the arrowheads. When she returned she said, "If she's so dangerous, we need to stop her."

"She and Thaddeus seem to be on better terms at the moment," I said. "Let's just hope it stays that way. She keeps talking about a guy named Östric. He must be their boss or something. I gather he must be at least as old as she is. I get the feeling that even if we get rid of her, someone else will come in to take her place. I feel like we're in the Twilight Zone."

Then my cell phone rang. Maribeth came out of the other room and stood in the entrance to the main gallery.

"Who is it?" she asked.

I looked at the caller I.D. "My dad."

"Answer it," she said, "I'll be right here listening." When she said the last word, the little pistol slid out of her sleeve and into her hand.

I tapped the phone. "Hey, dad!"

"Robbie, hey, how are things going?"

"Everything is fine here," I said.

"Really? I've been kind of concerned. You didn't call me yesterday like you said you would."

"Oh, yeah, sorry. I must have lost track of time. I've been busy with the museum."

Thaddeus came out of the office and stood next to Maribeth. He was wearing the new dress slacks, but that was all. He appeared confused and curious about my phone. "Is he talkin' to a person?"

Maribeth shushed him.

"I was just watching the news," dad said. "They had a story from Kinsville. Is it true there is a chimpanzee loose in town? Is that really what killed Carl?"

"They don't know for sure," I replied. "The detective stopped by and talked to me about it this morning."

"Don't you think you should have called me, son? Don't you think that's something I should know? You were supposed to keep me in the loop."

"I know," I said. "I'm sorry. I'll do better. I promise."

"Did the insurance people make it by yet?" dad asked.

107

"Not yet," I said. "The police just finished up this morning. Do you want me to give them a call?"

"I can do it," he said. "But you should have told me as soon as the police let you back into the building. What about Carl's funeral? Do you know if his family has made arrangements yet?"

"I don't know. I'm sorry. I'll check on that today."

Dad let out a heavy sigh. "I think I'll just cancel the rest of my appointments and head on back."

"No," I said. "We talked about this. You need to meet with these people. Listen, I'm sorry I've let you down. I promise I'll keep you informed from now on. I *promise*. You finish your trip, and I'll let you know the minute the insurance people arrive."

"And Carl's funeral," he added.

"That too."

"I'm counting on you, Robbie."

"I won't let you down."

Maribeth made a motion for me to end the call. I was just about to do that, but I got an idea. "Hey, dad, somebody was asking about one of our pieces today, and I was hoping you could help me with it." Maribeth scowled a warning and pointed her gun at me. I raised my hand for her to calm down.

"Sure," he replied. "What is it?"

"They said it was an old box with colored crystals inside or maybe crystals by themselves. I told them I'd never seen anything like that, but I'd ask you about it."

"Crystals?" he said. "No, I don't think so…oh wait…was it an elderly African American woman? Her last name started with an 'M'. Mrs. Masterson, I believe…or Masters…Massey. I can't remember exactly."

"That sounds right," I lied, trying to get him to spit it out.

"I forgot about her," he said. "She brought in a bucket of rocks for me to look at over a year ago. She said they belonged to her late husband and wanted me to tell her if they were

108

worth anything. It was mostly fossils—nothing too extraordinary—but I remember some small geodes or some quartz in there. I tried to tell her that I wasn't really qualified to appraise those things, but she wouldn't take no for an answer. She never came back for them, so I set them aside out of the way. I totally forgot about them until now."

"That sounds like them," I said. "So there wasn't a box?"

"No, just the bucket. Apologize to her for me. Tell her I tried to call her, but no one ever replied to my messages. She should take them down to the university and have someone there look at them. It's just not my expertise."

"Okay," I said. "But where are they? I haven't seen a bucket of rocks at all."

"Go into the front gallery there where it opens up to the gift shop. I put the bucket behind the pedestal that holds those two cannon balls. It's open in the back, and sometimes I stick things there to get them out of the way. It's next to the display case with the Civil War pieces. I just set them down and never went back to them. Tell her I'm sorry. I just have a lot going on."

"Okay. Thanks, dad. I'm sorry too about not calling you. Good luck with your meetings. I'll call you back tonight."

I ended the call and put the phone in my pocket. All eyes were on me. I didn't say anything right away.

"Well?" Maribeth said. "Where is this bucket of rocks?"

Now that I had some leverage, I was going to use it.

"First, put your gun away," I said. "Then give Thaddeus back that medallion."

Maribeth gave me a broad smile, "Are you feeling your oats, boy?"

"The name is Robert," I said. "Or you could call me Mr. Bright."

She chuckled and pushed the pistol back into her sleeve. "Fine. *Robert*. The gun is gone. Where is the bucket of rocks?"

"First give Thaddeus his medallion."

109

Thaddeus grinned at her.

"Did he tell you what the medallion does?" she asked.

"No," I said, suddenly feeling unsure about my demand. "It doesn't matter. He wants it back, so give it to him."

She opened her satchel and retrieved the medallion. She put the disc and chain into Thaddeus' open hand.

"You have forced me to go against Östric's orders. The only way he will forgive me now is if I return with the keys. If that bucket of rocks is merely rocks, I am not sure what I will do. Do you understand me? Boy?"

I understood. I walked through the main gallery toward Maribeth and Thaddeus like a man walking toward the executioner. Lacy followed, but she was a little confused. I tried to make eye contact with Maribeth, but I couldn't.

I passed through the gift shop then stopped just inside the small, front gallery. There was the open, broken case of artifacts from the American Civil War. To the right of that was the pedestal holding the two cannon balls from that same war.

"Dad said a woman wanted him to appraise some fossils and crystals for him," I said. "Makes sense they would be the keys, right?"

"Let's hope so for your sake," Maribeth replied.

Behind the cannon ball display, hidden away, was the gallon-sized, galvanized bucket.

"Thank you, God," I whispered. Then out loud I said, "Found it!"

I pulled it out. It was heavy. I carried it over to the counter by the cash register.

"Get out of my way," Maribeth said. "Let me look through them."

She forced herself through and grabbed the bucket. Then she gently turned it on its side then raked the rocks out onto the counter with her fingers. There were many fossils common to the region—mostly shell impressions and crinoids. As dad had said, "nothing too extraordinary."

There was a small, purple geode.

A piece of blue slag glass.

Then we all saw it—a piece of white crystal, about an inch long.

Maribeth and I grabbed for it at the same time, but I was faster. I snatched it away, clutched it tight in my fist, and held it up out of Maribeth's reach. As expected, her gun appeared again.

"I'm getting tired of this," she growled. "Give me the crystal!"

"I need an assurance you won't hurt or kill us after you get it," I said.

"You mean like this?" Maribeth said and shot Lacy in the leg.

CHAPTER 20

Lacy screamed and grabbed her left thigh.

"Maribeth! No!" Thaddeus yelled.

Blood soaked through Lacy's pants and spread, oozing between her fingers. She hopped then fell. Thaddeus knelt by her side and tried to pull her hand away.

I was stunned.

"Give me the crystal, or I'll put one in her other leg," Maribeth said, emotionless.

"Why would you do this?" I placed the small piece of crystal on the counter and dropped to my knees next to Lacy. I cradled her head.

"It hurts," Lacy cried.

"It's gonna be all right," Thaddeus reassured her. "I got my medallion, see?"

"I don't know what to do," I said. "Should I do a tourniquet, Lacy? How to I stop the blood?"

Thaddeus shoved his medallion in my face. "I have my medallion."

"Call an ambulance," Lacy whimpered.

I pulled out my phone. Then Thaddeus pried Lacy's hand away from her bleeding leg and pressed his medallion against the wound.

"What are you doing?" I asked.

"It will be all right, Miss Lacy," Thaddeus said. A blue light shone beneath his hand.

Lacy's expression changed. "It's vibrating. It doesn't hurt anymore. It kind of tickles."

"What's happening?" I asked.

The blue light dimmed. Thaddeus moved his hand and medallion. The bloody bullet rolled off the top of Lacy's leg to the floor. "The medallion can heal," he said. "We got to it fast enough, see? Pulled the bullet right out."

Lacy felt her leg again then stuck her finger into the hole in her pants. "He's right. I'm not bleeding anymore. I don't even think there is a scratch."

"Yeah, yeah, good as new," Maribeth said in an impatient and distracted tone. "Unfortunately, I don't think the medallions will heal this." She held the crystal she'd taken from Thaddeus in one hand and the crystal from the bucket in her other hand. "They do appear to be broken pieces of the same key."

I could not contain the loathing and rage I felt for the woman. I stood and got in her face. "How dare you! What is wrong with you?!"

"Now you have an idea about what the medallions can do," she said. "No harm done."

"No harm?!"

"Thaddeus, this little piece must be why you have been coming through here," she pondered aloud, ignoring me. "The key must be attracted to itself. Perhaps these two pieces will lead us to the third piece, and possibly the rest of the keys."

"I told you," Thaddeus said as he helped Lacy to her feet, "Emmet and Virgil had the other keys."

"Hey!" I yelled at Maribeth. "I'm talking to you!" She ignored me.

"They might not have the keys after all," she replied to Thaddeus. "You told me Virgil picked up two of the broken pieces of the white key, yet now here is one of them in my hand. We just need to find out who brought in the bucket of rocks."

When Lacy was standing again, she gave Maribeth an unexpected shove and pulled out her own gun. Maribeth took a couple of steps backward, caught her balance, and smirked.

"You'll be fine, girl," Maribeth said. "Be glad I didn't put it in your knee. That really would have hurt."

"How about I put one in *your* knee?!" Lacy yelled.

"You have a lot of fire," Maribeth replied. "You remind me of myself at your age."

I stepped between the two women and gently pushed down the end of Lacy's gun.

"Again with the gun?" I scolded.

"He's right," Maribeth said with an unconcerned chuckle. "Never pull it out if you aren't prepared to use it." She went back to the counter and moved the rocks around, hoping to find another piece of the key. "Okay, boy, tell the name of the woman who brought in these rocks. Maybe she has the rest of the keys."

"I don't know," I replied, and it was the truth. Even though my dad had just mentioned the woman's name, I couldn't come up with it.

"I don't believe you," she said with a cold stare. "Did your dad tell you the name?"

"Yes, but—"

"So your dad knows," she said. She studied the pieces of the key a moment. Then she lined up the two crystals so their ends touched. "Perhaps I should have an agent pay your dad a visit and ask him about it."

I grabbed her arm. "You leave my dad alone!"

There was a blue glow beneath her blouse. A white spark danced between the two crystals. Then the shorter of the two pulled against the longer like a magnet. The seam where they joined glowed with a brilliant white light.

Then Maribeth and I stood in a shaded alley between two buildings. There was dirt and sparse grass underfoot. One of the structures was built from rough planks and whitewashed. The other was made from logs. The whitewashed building had a door in the side which opened up to the alley, but it was closed at that moment.

"What just happened?" I said. "Where are we?"

"Keep your voice down," Maribeth replied wrenching her arm out of my grasp. "I do not know where we are. However, I suspect the key has brought us here...to itself. The missing piece and possibly the other keys could be nearby."

At one end of the alley was a manure pile almost as tall as I. The other end opened to a street paved with bricks. A man on a horse rode by. He was dressed similarly to the way Thaddeus was dressed the first time I saw him. There were more buildings in view on the other side of an open field. It was a little town.

"Did we just travel through time?" I whispered. "When I did this before, there were gurelachs everywhere."

"I told you I don't know where we are so I can't say whether we moved through time. I didn't see any of the monsters, but it is possible one got through with us. It is also possible we are in another world altogether." She held up the broken key. The two crystals were now one fused piece. It had repaired itself. "That is what the keys are supposed to do— open passage to other worlds."

"What world could it be? Is it familiar to you?"

She frowned at me and the manure pile. "It smells familiar. Do you see my satchel anywhere?"

"How many other worlds have you visited? Are they all similar?"

"I haven't visited any others," she said. "I know about the thirteen worlds only from what Östric has told me and from old books, and many of them were written from hearsay. The

115

keys have been hidden for millennia. No one has intentionally traveled between worlds in that time so far as I know."

"Thaddeus said that the gates open up naturally sometimes."

"It does happen, but it is very rare and a completely random occurrence. The people get stuck wherever they wind up."

Two horses pulling a wagon passed. The back was loaded with burlap bags, plump with grain. We were not noticed.

"Where ever or whenever we are, I am certain we are not dressed properly," she said.

I wore jeans, white Nikes, and a blue Star Trek T-shirt with Spock on the front.

"You're better off than I am," I said.

"Not really," she replied. "As Thaddeus pointed out earlier, this skirt would be much too short and considered obscene if we are in eighteen seventy-seven. You could take off your shirt and attract less attention."

I did take off my shirt, but I turned it backwards and put it on again.

"Let me have your suit jacket," I said.

"It's too small for you."

"It'll be fine until I can find us both something else to wear. I need to cover up this T-shirt."

She removed her jacket. The contraption on her arm that held her spring-loaded sleeve gun looked like it would be uncomfortable. I almost remarked about it, but then I noticed her other weapon. Hanging from a strap connected to the waistband of her skirt was a golden crescent.

"You have an astra too?" I asked.

"Many agents of the Ancients carry astrae."

"Who are the Ancients?"

"Shhh," she whispered, putting a finger over her mouth. "Listen."

There were voices coming from inside the whitewashed building. Maribeth handed me her jacket then walked over to the closed door and put her ear to it. I tiptoed behind her.

"What is it?" I asked.

"I know that voice," she replied. She bent over, lifted each foot to remove her high heels, and turned to me. "Put the jacket on and go around to the front entrance. We'll take them by surprise." Then the mechanism on her arm sprang to life, and the pistol leapt into her hand.

"What am I supposed to do? Will they be armed? I don't have a weapon."

"Just go through the front and distract them so I get inside unnoticed. You let me worry about the weapons."

"But—"

"Remember, I'm your only way home, so don't get any ideas about turning against me."

"But—"

"Go," she said

I nodded and struggled into her jacket. It was tight across the shoulders, and the sleeves were short and bit into my armpits. I hoped I wouldn't be pressed into a fight, because even if I knew how to fight, my range of motion had just been limited. The faint scent of her perfume was nice, but after the way she had treated us, particularly Lacy, I didn't allow myself to linger on how good Maribeth smelled or how pretty she was.

I jogged to the front corner of the building, shielded my eyes in the bright sunlight and looked both ways. To my left was the log building and past that were a couple of empty lots then another row of short buildings. To my right and ahead was the little town. People and horses and wagons moved around in the streets. Judging by the style of clothing and hats, it was the mid to late 1800's. It was Kinsville, I recognized the courthouse.

"If only dad could see this," I said. I wanted to take a quick picture with my phone.

117

"Go!" Maribeth hissed.

I gave her a "thumbs up", and stepped up onto the wooden porch of the whitewashed building. There were two large windows in the front, but the curtains prevented me from seeing inside. There was no placard to indicate what sort of building it was. For all I knew, I was about to walk into someone's home. I considered knocking, but no—Maribeth wanted a distraction.

CHAPTER 21

I pulled the latch and the door swung open on creaking hinges. There were tables against the walls on either side of me. On the table to my right were several pairs of shoes and boots, most of them dirty and worn. The table to my left was the work station of a cobbler. No one was in sight.

"Hello?" I said.

"Howdy," said a man's voice from the back room. "Be right there."

I waited for Maribeth to make her move. A short balding man with wire rimmed glasses and a leather apron entered and gave me a polite smile.

"Good day, young sir," he said. "How may I assist you?"

"Is this a cobbler shop?" I asked.

He looked around and chuckled. "Seems to be. I also do tanning and leather work. I can do repairs on shoes and other leather goods." Then his eyes widened at my Nikes. "Well, I never! Where did you get shoes like that?"

I groaned and tried to think of a plausible story. "Oh, well...um...they came mail order from Boston. They are the newest thing in modern fashion."

119

"Hmph," he said. "Just goes to prove Yankees are crazy as coots. And what would possess you to want to own a pair? Are you tryin' to be a fancy dandy?"

"Well, they're running shoes so—"

"Where're ya runnin' to? Is the law after ya?"

"No, sir."

Then another man stepped in from the back room. He wore much finer clothes. I put him at about thirty years old. He had a dark mustache which curved down and connected with thick sideburns. He was the same height as the cobbler, but his top hat made him appear taller.

"Shall we finish our business, Mr. Langston?" the newcomer said to the cobbler then gave me a curt nod. He had the diluted accent of a British expatriate.

"Apologies, Mr. Strathmore," the cobbler replied. "I was just speakin' with this young man about his shoes. Have you ever seen such?"

The man in the hat frowned at my feet. "I cannot say that I have."

"Fancy dandies," the cobbler said, shaking his head.

"About our business…" Mr. Strathmore said.

"Yes, of course," the cobbler said and pried his eyes away from my futuristic footwear. Then he addressed me again. "I will return shortly, young man, after Mr. Strathmore and I have settled up."

The door opened in the back. Then Maribeth rushed in behind them and stuck her gun in Strathmore's back.

"Oh dear!" said Langston the cobbler and backed up until he sat hard on a stool in the corner.

"Where is the box, Virgil?" Maribeth sneered.

The man in the top hat was unfazed. Without turning around, he raised both hands and grinned. "Is that you, Maribeth? Did Östric get impatient and send you to check up on us?"

"You could say that," she replied. "Where is the box?"

"Do you know what is in that box, my dear?" he asked.

"I do," she replied. "But you shouldn't know. Did you open it?"

"Thaddeus opened it," he replied. "I merely looked inside."

"Where is it?"

"Thaddeus has it," he said with a shrug. "He stole it. I wired you about that last week. I told you he couldn't be trusted."

This confirmed my suspicions that we were in 1877.

"Thaddeus says you have it," Maribeth said.

The man turned slightly trying to get a look at her, but she goaded him harder with the gun.

"Have you spoken with Thaddeus?" he asked.

"I spoke with him no more than half an hour ago," she replied. "Does that surprise you?"

"Ah," he said with the tone of realization, "so this is why I have a gun in my back."

"Perhaps I should go," the cobbler announced from the corner. "You two obviously have a private matter to discuss, and the young lady is without her dress, and if my wife arrived I would never be able to explain—"

"Shut up," Maribeth barked.

"You are without your dress, Maribeth?" Virgil Strathmore said with delight. "I *must* see this."

"You'll keep your eyes on the boy," she said and shoved her hand into the pocket of his coat.

"Is the lad a friend of yours?" Strathmore asked her, sizing me up. "One of your playthings?"

She pulled a Derringer from his pocket and tossed it to me. I caught it like a hot potato.

"Hold onto that for me," she told me. I felt awkward with it, so I stuck it into my back pocket.

Maribeth's hand moved around the front of his coat and dipped into his vest pocket. She came out with a small gold disc. It was smaller than the medallion Thaddeus had, and there was no crystal in the center. She tossed it to me. On one side was a woman's profile, and on the other was an eagle. The date stamped on the head's side was 1870.

"A ten-dollar gold piece," I said with awe. There was a picture of a coin like it in one of my dad's appraisal guides at the museum. I had often daydreamed of finding coins like this as buried treasure when I was a kid. In 1877 that coin had a face value of ten dollars, but in my time it would be worth thousands. "What do I do with it?" I asked.

"Hang onto it for now," she said.

"Are you robbing me, Maribeth?" Virgil said.

"Please, ma'am," Mr. Langston pleaded. "Thou shalt not steal. It is the eighth commandment."

"And thou shalt not speak!" Maribeth said and gave the cobbler a nasty scowl. She pushed her hand into another pocket. She grinned and pulled out the third piece of the white crystal key. It was as large as the other two pieces combined.

"What's this?" she said.

"You know what it is," Virgil replied. "If you have spoken with Thaddeus, I am sure you got the information out of him. I am familiar with your tactics."

"Where are the other keys?"

"I do not have them," he said.

"But you know where they are. Are they with Emmet McCain?"

He didn't answer.

Maribeth pressed the pistol into his back once more. "You have until the count of three to tell me where you and Emmet hid the box and the rest of the keys, or I will shoot you where you stand. One—"

"Ma'am, oh please ma'am, no!" The cobbler cried. "The sixth commandment! Thou shalt not kill! Not in my shop!"

"Two—"

"I have nothing to tell you," was Virgil Strathmore's dignified reply.

"Three!"

She fired the gun into his back and the bullet exited his chest with a flutter of his lapel. I gasped in surprise and took a step back. Virgil's mouth flopped open, his eyes went vacant, his head lolled, and he crumpled to the floor onto his face. His hat rolled and came to rest in front of my "fancy dandies". I looked up at the cobbler to see what he would do, but he had fainted.

CHAPTER 22

"Why did you kill him?" I said to Maribeth. "He didn't tell you where the keys were."

"He's not dead," she said and knelt beside his body. "I knocked the wind out of him good, but he won't die, not from that. He's an agent. His medallion will mend him. Come on. Help me remove his coat and pants while he's unconscious."

"What for?" I asked and picked up his hat.

"I can wear his pants and hat," she said. "Maybe I'll pass for a man until we get pulled back or finish our business here."

"I doubt that," I said. "You're too…too…womanly."

She grinned, "That's sweet, boy. Now come help me before he bleeds on them too much. You can wear his coat. It should fit you better than mine."

I joined her, and I tugged at Virgil's coat while she worked on his pants. When I got his coat off, I found his astra hidden in a special wide pocket in the lining. I pulled it out and gripped it with the points of the crescent aimed away from me.

"So these things shoot lasers or something?"

Maribeth gave me an annoyed look and took it from me then placed it on the floor next to her own astra. "They are energy weapons, but not lasers. Check to make sure there are no more secret pockets in his coat."

124

"There aren't," I said. I took her suit jacket off, handed it back to her. Then I used a rag from the cobbler's workbench to dab up the blood on Virgil's coat before I put it on. The jacket was snug, but it was a better fit.

"Help me roll him over," she said. "Then go over there and see if you can find a pair of shoes that will fit you."

When we turned him over, his medallion shined through the fabric of his shirt. "Will that heal everything? Will it bring people back from the dead?"

"No," was her reply as she finished removing his pants.

When she didn't elaborate, I said, "Okay. Is there a reason why I'm changing shoes? Are we going somewhere?"

"Yep. Virgil is going to take us to get the box."

She stood, unzipped her skirt and let it drop to the floor. My jaw dropped with it. Stockings, garter belt, knife strapped to her bare thigh....

"Rein in those teenage hormones," she said and reached for Virgil's pants. "Believe it or not, your ogling is making me uncomfortable."

"Sorry." I felt the blood rush into my face and turned away to the table of shoes.

Then Mr. Langston the cobbler stirred. When he saw Maribeth, now even more undressed and bent over in front of him, his eyes bugged out. I thought he might faint again.

"Lead me not into temptation," he prayed. "Deliver me from evil."

"Good," Maribeth said. "You're awake." She pulled on Virgil's pants and turned to face the cobbler. "Why was he here? What sort of business did he have with you?"

Mr. Langston glanced down at Virgil's body. "Is he dead?"

"What business?" Maribeth repeated.

"I made him a tool roll," he said with a quivering voice. "He was in to pick it up and pay me."

"A tool roll? Did he say what it was for?"

"No, but it must have been for some dandy tools. He wanted all the pouches made a particular size, and he had me line it all with rabbit fur."

Maribeth shook her head in confusion and said, "Go get it for me."

The man hopped up and rushed to obey her. He returned with a roll of dyed leather tied up with thongs. He presented it to Maribeth and backed away. She untied the straps and unrolled the wide strip of leather onto the table.

There were seven narrow pouches sewn side by side inside the roll. The whole thing was lined with gray and white fur. Maribeth caressed the soft fur then stuck a finger into one of the pouches. She was trying to figure out its purpose. It was apparent to me.

"It's for the keys," I said impatiently. "He had it made to carry the crystals."

She pulled out the piece she had taken from Virgil's pocket and slid it into one of the pouches. It was a perfect fit.

"You do nice work, Mr. Langston," she said. "We'll take it. We'll also need two pairs of shoes."

"Take whatever you want," he said. "Just do me no harm. I have a family."

"Do you have a wagon and a horse?"

"There's a buckboard and an old mare out back," he nodded.

Maribeth snapped her fingers at me. "Pay the man."

I sighed and relinquished the ten dollar gold piece.

Half an hour later, Maribeth, in her new top hat and trousers, drove the buckboard north out of town. It was a slow and bumpy way to travel. I sat in the back to guard Virgil Strathmore. The man was still unconscious, in his underwear, and his hands were tied behind his back with hemp rope. His medallion continued to glow to heal his wound. We had him covered over with a canvas tarp so no one could see what we

126

were hauling. We had left Mr. Langston tied up in his shop to prevent him from fetching the sheriff before we had a chance to get away.

I stared at the old boots on my feet. They were uncomfortable, and there was a hole in the sole of the right one as big as a quarter. They had been a job Mr. Langston had not yet repaired. They were the only pair that fit me. My white Nikes sat next to me.

"Where are we going?" I asked Maribeth.

"Some place secluded. I need to question Virgil when he wakes up."

"By question do you mean torture?"

"I mean question…with the possibility of torture."

"I can't be a part of anything like that," I said.

"Virgil has heard stories about me. I won't need to hurt him so long as he believes I am capable of hurting him, and he knows I am capable, because I already shot him. It is the anticipation and dread that will make him talk."

"But if he's one of these agents, hasn't he been trained to endure stuff like that?"

"Somewhat," she replied. "But he believes me to be especially brutal."

"Is it true? Are you brutal?"

"As I said, I don't need to be brutal so long as he believes I am."

"That doesn't really answer my question," I said.

"I know."

We travelled in silence for a while. I was struck by how quiet the world was. The air smelled differently too. We passed by a little house, and I waved to the woman who was scrubbing clothes outside next to a cauldron of water. I pulled out my phone and snapped a picture.

"Stop that," Maribeth said. "You'll attract attention."

I returned the phone to my pocket. "I probably missed my only opportunity to get a picture of old Kinsville earlier. I should have climbed up on the roof and taken a panorama. Dad would have loved to see the whole town."

"You would have gotten us arrested or lynched or affected the timeline in a negative way."

"What makes you think our interaction with Mr. Langston hasn't changed things?" I said.

"It might have, but the keys are too important not to take the chance. Your photo op would have been a reckless frivolity."

"I practically grew up in a museum. All dad ever talks about is the past. Now, here I am in the past. I don't see this as frivolous at all. I could bring my dad back all sorts of details about this time period. I could even bring back an important item that—"

"No," she interrupted. "Absolutely not. With the exception of the keys, we must do our best not to bring anything back with us. Östric warned me about the problems associated with time travel, and that was one of them."

"Who is this Östric guy anyway?" I asked.

"Östric is one of the Ancients."

"And?"

"I am not sure how much Thaddeus has told you. You already know more than you should."

"Then what's the harm in giving me the full scoop? I know about gurelachs. Thaddeus told me about portals into alternate universes and stuff."

"Did he tell you that? That doesn't sound like verbiage Thaddeus would use."

"Not really, but that's how I understood it."

"Yes, well," she said. "I am sure it all sounds like science fiction or magic."

I climbed over the back of the bench and sat next to her. "So tell me."

She cast an annoyed glance over her shoulder.

"Don't worry about him," I said. "I'll keep an eye on Virgil. Tell me everything. I have to know what's going on."

CHAPTER 23

Maribeth slouched there with the reins in her hands, eyes straight ahead, swaying with the movement of our ride. She was quiet for so long, I was about to give up on getting the truth out of her, but then she spoke.

"The Ancients are a long-lived race of people known as the Nepheel. At one time they controlled travel between the thirteen worlds, and I suppose they still do in a way."

"Nepheel," I repeated the word because it was familiar to me. "Where have I heard that before?"

She shrugged, "They were written about in ancient texts — legends and folklore mostly, but there is truth to the stories. They are called by different names, but the closest in pronunciation is Nephilim."

"Are you one?" I asked. "Back at the museum, you said you were old."

"No, I am not, but they have enabled me to have long life because I work for them."

"How long?"

She hesitated but decided to answer. "I was born in sixteen fifty-one in New Amsterdam. My parents died when I was a baby. I don't even remember my last name. Agents found me in a church where I was being cared for by a priest. I began training to serve the Ancients when I was ten."

"Whoa. Hundreds of years," I stated. "You are *hundreds* of years old?"

"The Ancients live for *thousands* of years," she said. "I will never live that long. The medallion heals and slows aging, but it does not make me immortal or invincible."

"Still...I need to get me one of those medallions," I chuckled.

"Not likely," she said. "The Ancients are very strict. An agent must prove their loyalty and usefulness for many years before they earn their medallion. The Ancients are careful with whom they share their technology. And yes, it is technology, not magic."

"Alien technology? Do they come from another planet—one of the other twelve worlds?"

"The thirteen worlds are not different planets; they are different manifestations of the same planet. The worlds occupy the same space, but in different frequencies."

"Ah," I said. "So I was right. I saw a show about that on public television. It's multiple universes, the multiverse. Comic books are full of that stuff too—parallel worlds, alternate realities, other dimensions. They say there are an infinite number of them."

She shook her head. "The thirteen are distinct worlds. There are other worlds on this plane, but they are variations of the thirteen. However, the number of variants is not infinite. No more than fifty-six exist, I believe."

"What is it that you do for the Nepheel?"

"Whatever they need me to do. Östric has a few hundred people around the world acting on his behalf. Not all do the same sort of job as Thaddeus and I."

She turned again to inspect the tarp.

"He hasn't moved at all," I said. "Maybe he didn't make it."

131

"He'll be fine. The bullet went through his lung, and it will take longer to heal than your friend's leg. We'll stop in those woods ahead and wait for his medallion to finish its work. He's probably had worse injuries."

"How long have you known him?"

"He was relatively new to the work at this time," she said. "He came on during the eighteen forties. He was an orphan like me, if my memory serves. We worked together on two jobs during the Civil War. We helped recruit Thaddeus at that time. Virgil was an efficient and effective agent. He disappeared just like Thaddeus in eighteen seventy-seven. Emmet did too."

"We know where Thaddeus wound up," I said. "What about this guy? What happens...or happened...to him?"

"Don't know," she shrugged. "All this time, we presumed they had been killed and the keys stolen even though there were never any bodies. There was always the possibility Virgil and Emmet used the keys to open a passage to one of the other worlds. Östric says the keys have to be in specific locations to work, but we've already seen what happened with the white key, so I don't know."

"Why did these men have the keys at all? Were they stolen?"

"It's a long story, but I'll try to give you the condensed version.

"For thousands of years, there was a great deal of traffic between the thirteen worlds. Earth was the hub. It was connected to the other twelve worlds, but they were not connected to each other. Earth was sort of like the Silk Road of inter-world trade at that time. All movement had to pass through Earth, and it was all controlled by the Nepheel.

"Around eleven thousand years ago, for whatever reason—I suspect there must have been a disagreement over the Nepheel's rules or trade tariffs— but for whatever reason, a group of traders from the world of Otnuk attempted to circumvent Earth and the Nepheel by creating a direct passage

132

to the world of Vehala using technology they had stolen from the Nepheel. They succeeded in opening the gateway between the worlds, but they also inadvertently opened a gateway to the lower plane which was previously unknown."

"Is the lower plane not part of the thirteen worlds? Is it part of those fifty or so variants you mentioned?"

"No. The lower plane is something different and up to that point had not been connected with our plane of existence or even known about. The gateway the traders of Otnuk opened between themselves and Vehala and the lower plane came to be known as The Gape, and no one on Otnuk could close it. Armies from the lower plane worlds of Sheol and Jeoke, led by a being named Bahal, pushed through The Gape into Otnuk and Vehala.

"Over the course of several decades, Otnuk and Vehala were overrun, and armies of the lower plane began to attack Earth through the open gates it shared with those two worlds. There were battles on Earth and the Nepheel were nearly wiped out. Realizing the enemy was too strong and great, and to prevent the invasion from spreading to the rest of the thirteen worlds, the decision was made to close all of the gates between all of the worlds. This stranded travelers, traders, even armies from other worlds on Earth.

"The five hundred or so Nepheel who were left collected the keys and some other important items and went into hiding to prevent the gates from being opened again until it was safe. The keys were lost over time due to infighting between different families and factions of the Nepheel. Then, in the early eighteen sixties, the keys along with some other artifacts were discovered again in a cave in Colorado by gold prospectors. The Smithsonian Institute acquired them. Östric has agents working in the Institute and found out about the discovery. He sent additional agents to take them and bring them back to him. Thaddeus, Virgil, and Emmet were those agents."

133

We entered the woods and stopped.

"That is one crazy story," I said.

"And all of it true," Maribeth said and hopped, down out of the wagon. "It's been a while since I drove a rig like this. If I had known I would need to use the skill again, I would have spent some time among the Amish to brush up."

"I hope telling me all of this doesn't get you into trouble with your boss."

"The only way he would find out I told you is if you went public with it, and you aren't stupid enough to do that, are you? Even if you did, no one would believe it. There are some people who have put similar information on websites, but for the most part they are labeled as nuts. Östric might order me to kill you or recruit you if he found out you knew. Since you don't seem to be agent material, I would probably kill you."

"Why would you kill me?! Why wouldn't I be agent material? I could be an agent."

"Nah, you're too soft, and you have too many attachments. Being an agent of the Ancients is a lifetime commitment, and the lifetime is long, measured in centuries. You have to be willing to do anything they tell you. I don't think you are cut out for it."

She walked around to the back of the wagon and threw the canvas tarp aside. Virgil was awake, but groggy. His medallion was dark. It was attached to a rawhide cord around his neck. She pulled it over his head and handed it to me.

"It's not yours to keep," she said. "But put it on for the time being in case we have trouble. It will give you some protection."

"Maribeth?" Virgil said in a feeble voice. "Why are you wearing my hat?"

On one side of the golden disc, raised on the surface, were overlapping circles.

"This symbol," I said. "I have seen it before."

"It is fairly common. It is usually called the Flower of Life. It is used to represent different things in different cultures and belief systems—the start and renewal of life, the interconnectedness of things, that sort of thing. The Nepheel accept all those meanings and a few others. They also use it to represent the Octave worlds. Earth is the center circle and the other circles are other worlds."

"But there are only seven circles here. I thought there were suppose to be thirteen."

"The Octave worlds were the primary worlds in the eyes of the Nepheel, because those worlds were directly under their influence—part of their empire so to speak. The Gradi worlds were secondary and not included in the basic symbol. But I have seen this symbol extended out to include not only the Octave worlds but the Gradi and Variant worlds as well."

She grabbed Virgil's ankles and dragged him out of the wagon. He landed with a thump and suddenly became more alert.

"Come now, Maribeth," he said. "There is no call for this sort of treatment."

"Your treatment is about to get a whole lot worse," she said.

CHAPTER 24

Maribeth put a boot on Virgil's chest, right on the bloody spot where the bullet had exited. "Tell me where the box is, and we can avoid any more unpleasantness."

"Whatever Thaddeus told you is a lie," he said. "I don't have the keys."

"You had a piece of one. He didn't lie about that."

"Thaddeus stole it, and I stopped him. The key was broken in the scuffle."

Maribeth pushed her foot harder against his chest.

"I want to believe you, Virgil," she said. "I want to believe that you and Emmet haven't gone off on your own. Thaddeus suspects you might even be doing work for one of the other families."

"Thaddeus is a scoundrel. I am offended that you would take his word over mine especially after the way he two-timed you!"

She bent over and punched him in the mouth. He swallowed his cry and turned his face away.

"Stop it!" I yelled.

"Hush up, boy," she said. Then she spoke again to Virgil. "Without your medallion this is going to hurt a lot more, and it's not going to heal."

"Good," he spat back, through bloody lips and teeth. "I shall be out of my misery before long."

"Oh, I won't let you off that easy. You know my reputation. I can stretch this out for days. All you have to do to keep it from happening is tell me where to find the keys, and I'll untie you and return your medallion and astra. All will be forgiven."

Virgil laughed, "You shoot me and beat on me then talk about forgiveness?"

"Shoot you, beat on you, cut on you, burn you — whatever it takes to loosen your tongue."

"Please," I said. "I really don't want to be a part of torture. Can't we resolve this in a civilized manner?"

They both blinked at me.

"Where did you find this one, Maribeth?" Virgil grinned. "Miss Nancy's Finishing School for Etiquette and Grace?"

Maribeth joined him in a chuckle. "He told me earlier he wanted to be an agent. Can you imagine?"

"I said no such thing," I insisted. "But I'm glad the two of you can have a laugh together at my expense."

Maribeth lifted her foot from Virgil's chest then squatted next to him.

"I'll make a deal with you, Virgil, for the sake of the boy's weak constitution. As it stands right now, Östric believes it was Thaddeus that betrayed him. Since Thaddeus is no longer with us, it would be easy to let Östric go on believing that."

"What do you mean Thaddeus is no longer with us? Did he defect or...something else? What did you do to Thaddeus?"

"It doesn't matter," she said. "All that matters is that you not get on Östric's bad side the way Thaddeus did. Maybe you've been telling the truth. Maybe you and Emmet were protecting the keys from Thaddeus. If that's so, then we can go meet Emmet right now, get the keys, and catch the next train out of this ugly little town."

Virgil didn't speak. Either he was being uncooperative, or he was thinking it over.

"The cobbler gave me the tool roll," Maribeth added. "I know you had it made to smuggle the keys. That doesn't look good, but I can forget about it." She pulled out a knife. I presumed it had been the one I'd seen strapped to her thigh in the cobbler's shop. "Or I can cut off your fingers a knuckle at a time, heal them back with a medallion, cut them off again, and heal them back again. How many times do you think I would have to do that until you finally talked to me?"

The two stared at each other, poker-faced.

Finally, Virgil let out a defeated sigh and said, "I can see why you're Östric's favorite. The truth is Emmet and I were contacted by one of the other families after we got the box."

"Which family?"

"Does it matter?" he said. "They have offered us a fortune for the keys, and they gave us some money in earnest."

"Östric provides everything you need or desire," Maribeth said. "Why would an offer like that even tempt you?"

"Emmet and I have been thinking we might like to get out—go our own ways. We knew if we told Östric, he would cut us off and take away our medallions, if he let us leave or live at all. This other family promised us the freedom we desired with wealth and long life to boot, all in exchange for the keys. It seemed like a good trade."

"How did they even know you had the keys?"

"Word gets around," Virgil said with a shrug. "The other families knew about the Smithsonian acquisition, or at least some of them did. That's why Östric sent three of us; it was a dangerous mission. We were attacked by assassins in the National Mall after we left the Smithsonian with the package. We barely escaped. Östric kept us in the dark about the package, but we knew it must be something important. Thaddeus was the first to guess what it was and opened the box to confirm it. That's when Emmet and I decided it was our time."

"Aren't you concerned about what will happen when one of the other families gets the keys?"

"I have no more concern than giving them to Östric. I think those keys are a danger to the world."

"And Thaddeus didn't want to play along?"

He shrugged. "He must have suspected something or got his own offer, because he took the box. When we caught up with him here in Kinsville and took it back, we found one of the keys was missing. That's when it came to blows."

Maribeth stood, went to the wagon, and returned with the tool roll. She unrolled it on the ground and pulled the piece of crystal from one of the pouches.

"This is the piece I took from you," she said. Then she reached in her pocket and pulled out the fused crystals from Thaddeus and the museum.

"Is that the piece Thaddeus got after our fight?"

"Yes," Maribeth answered, "plus another. They joined together again when I placed them end to end."

"Another? The crystal broke only into three pieces. Thaddeus grabbed one, and I grabbed the other two. I gave one to Emmet as a sign of our partnership. How did you get Emmet's piece?"

"She got it from me," I offered.

Virgil jerked his head at me, and his eyebrows shot up. "From you? And how did Miss Nancy here get his hands on Emmet's piece?"

Maribeth held the two pieces up in each hand. "I have been thinking about this since we arrived here," she said, turning to address me. "The whole reason Thaddeus kept appearing at the museum was because a piece of the key was there to pull him through. It was attracted to itself—no doubt activated by the lightning during the storm. Now that we have all three pieces here with us...."

139

The realization hit me hard. "Are you saying that since all the pieces of the key are here, we're stuck in eighteen seventy-seven? We can't go back?"

"It is likely," she said.

"What are you babbling about?" Virgil said.

"Technically, we do have Emmet's piece of the white key," she continued. "Somehow it wound up in that bucket of rocks in the museum more than a century from now. However, it isn't in that bucket yet, is it? At this point in time in eighteen seventy-seven, it is in Emmet's possession. That means two identical pieces of that key now exist in this time. If it pulled us through time to find itself, then why not pull us through space for the same purpose?"

"Huh?" was all I could come up with.

"It hasn't been working properly because it was damaged," she said. "It first had to come together, whole. The lightning from the storm sort of woke it up or gave it the jump start it needed to power up—I don't know—then it began the process of healing itself, no doubt aided by the medallions. If we want to get back, we'll have to break it again and separate the pieces. We'll have to put a piece of it where we know it will get the power it needs from the lightning during that storm. We'll have to hide a piece of it in the gristmill."

"Okay," I said. "Let's do it. Let's go now."

"No," she said. "First I need it to take me to Emmet. I have to get the other keys."

She held the fused piece of crystal close to the piece she had taken from Virgil Strathmore. A white light sparked between them. The medallion hanging around her neck glowed blue, and she vanished.

CHAPTER 25

Virgil, in his dirty white union suit, hands still bound behind his back, rolled up and sat. He grinned and said, "Dash it, boy, but I do believe she has been translated. She's off to one of the other worlds. I can't say I am displeased. She would have tormented me until I begged for death."

"No, the key has taken her to the other piece of itself," I said. "To Emmet."

"But you said *you* had Emmet's piece of the key."

"Emmet has two pieces," I told him rather than explain the time travel and duplication of the piece of crystal.

Virgil's brow furrowed. "Is that so? Well now. Does he have another partner I don't know about? Could be that he and Thaddeus are in cahoots."

"Listen, the key has transported Maribeth to wherever Emmet is. Now that she is there, she will take the other keys from Emmet and go to Östric. I need you to get me there now. Maribeth is my only way home."

Virgil shook his head. "Maribeth cares nothing for you. Maribeth cares about Maribeth. If she is with Emmet, then my deal with him is a bust. By the time I get there, Emmet will have told her where he hid the keys. Maribeth will kill him and be gone. Bounties will be on my head from two different Nepheel families. I think it is best if you give me my medallion so I can take my leave of this place—cut my losses. At least I still have my share of the earnest money."

"No, you take me to find Emmet. You don't get this medallion back until after I have been reunited with Maribeth."

"Well, looky at Miss Nancy trying to sprout himself some plums," Virgil needled. Then he scowled. "Lad, get over here and untie me. I've had enough of your impertinence."

I would have to untie him. Even if I got him back into the wagon and forced him to tell me how to get to Emmet, I wouldn't know how to drive the thing.

"Untie me now, I say!" He rocked back and kicked his bare feet in the air then stomped the leaf-covered ground like a toddler having a tantrum.

I sighed and leaned against the back of the wagon. Virgil rolled again and attempted to stand. He struggled and cursed but couldn't make it to his feet.

"There still might be time for you to save Emmet," I reasoned. "I need you to work with me."

"I don't give a tinker's damn about Emmet nor you," he replied as he rolled toward a tree.

"What about the rest of the fortune? If you get the keys before Emmet breaks and tells Meribeth, you could get his share."

He stopped and considered what I'd said. Then he rolled once more and used the tree as a brace to push himself up. He stood, hunched over and out of breath. Dried leaves and bits of grass and dirt stuck to his clothes and hung from his hair and sideburns.

"Emmet and I are to deliver the box and the complete set of keys," he said between breaths. "The white key was broken. We divided up the rest to keep each other honest whilst I went away to do business with the cobbler. I have no knowledge of where Emmet hid his portion. I know not what the other family will do to me if I deliver half."

"All the more reason to take us to Emmet!" I said. "Are we far from him?"

"I could not say without knowing where we are now," he replied.

"A few minutes north of Kinsville off the main road."

"Shouting distance?" he asked.

"What? No, we're farther from town than that."

"Good," he grinned. "Then they won't hear you scream."

He roared and charged with his shoulder down. Before I could react, his blow caught me in the ribs and knocked me off my feet. I hit the ground hard. He grunted as he scrambled to regain his footing. I tried to blink away the stars and catch my breath so I could stand, but he was on me again. He straddled me, reared back and slammed his forehead into mine.

There was blinding pain then darkness.

When I awoke, it was I who was in my underwear and under the tarp. The sun was still out, and under the canvas, I was uncomfortably warm. I felt the movement of the wagon and the throbbing of my skull.

Virgil was singing loudly and badly, "*It rained all night the day I left, the weather it was dry! The sun so hot, I froze to death — Suzanna don't you cry!*"

I had no idea how long I had been unconscious or how he had managed to get out of the rope. I tried to sit up but couldn't.

"*Oh! Suzanna! Don't you cry for me!*"

I tried again, and there was a sharp catch in my side, which surprised me, and I cried out.

"*I come from Alabama with a banjo*—huh? You awake back there, lad?"

My only reply was a moan. There was a moment where the only sound was the creaking of the wagon wheels and clop, clop, clop of the horse hooves on the packed dirt road.

Then Virgil said, "I must humbly apologize for my treatment of you. I was a belligerent cuss back there, but it was only because Maribeth had me riled, and I knew not who you were. I think if you get to know me, you will find me to be a polite sort. I think the two of us can do business together. It would be beneficial for someone other than the Nepheel to have control over the keys."

I managed to squeak out a hesitant, "Okay?"

He continued. "I could have left you tied to a tree. I could have covered you in molasses and let the ants and other critters have you. I would have too—I like to do that sort of thing—except when I was taking your clothes, I noticed your odd looking drawers, and you had words on the back of your shirt: *'You'd better Trek yourself before you wreck yourself.'* I don't know what that means, but there was that painting of a man in a military uniform—he had pointed ears, and he made a distinctive salute with his hand. I have seen the drawings in the Ancients' texts. I know this race with pointed ears comes from one of the Gradi worlds. I also found this." He held up my phone. "I can only presume you are one of their ambassadors or agents."

"Give me that," I said.

"I will keep it for now. My hope is you can provide me safe passage and sanctuary to your world. Then I will return your...item."

I couldn't think of anything to say, so I replied, "Okay."

"Good," he said. "Very good. We are approaching Kinsville. You keep yourself hidden under the covering until we are through the town, and after we have passed, I will use my medallion to heal that knot on your head."

I reached up to my throat to find the medallion missing. The movement of my arm caused my side to hurt again.

"I think you broke my ribs," I said.

"We'll heal that too," he added.

"Why didn't you heal me already? My head is killing me."

"I had to wait until after you and I had our parley. Surely you understand the need to keep you incapacitated."

"Sure," I grunted. "Whatever."

"And now, my boy, the time has come for your silence."

There were distant voices, the braying of a donkey, the bleating of goats. We were entering Kinsville.

"Good day to you, sir!" Virgil called out to someone on the street. Then he mumbled something indiscernible either to himself or to the horse.

There was a change in the sound of the hooves and wheels as we moved over a section of road that was paved with stones or bricks.

"A fine day, ma'am," Virgil said to someone else. I imagined him reaching to tip his hat only to remember it was missing.

We moved back onto dirt. The braying donkey was louder. There were more voices and laughter. There was hammering, a slamming door, and a small bell. Soon the sounds diminished as we moved away from them. Finally, we slowed and stopped. Virgil pulled away the canvas tarp and gave me a nod. He wore his own coat and my jeans. I was taller than he, so the pant legs were rolled up.

"I am pleased we did not have an encounter with the town's sheriff considering we are in possession of a stolen horse," he said. "It would have further escalated matters when he discovered you. I would have swung from the gallows by tomorrow morning."

He removed his medallion and put it against my head. I felt a tingling and saw nothing but blue light. Soon the pain was gone. The glow faded.

He moved the medallion to my side. I winced.

145

"What about clothes?" I asked. "I can't be out in my underwear."

He reached down in the wagon near my head, grabbed a pile of rags then dropped them on my lap.

"While you slept, we passed a woman doing laundry," he said. "She agreed to part with these in trade for your shoes."

"You didn't give her my Nikes, did you?"

"If you are referring to those white shoes from your world, the answer is no. I gave the pair from your feet—the ones you stole from the cobbler."

"I paid for those shoes," I said.

"With *my* gold," he replied.

The clothes Virgil had traded for my holey shoes were indeed rags.

"These aren't even clean," I said as I pulled the lace-up shirt over my head. "They stink. I'll probably wind up with lice."

"Yes," he agreed with a sympathetic frown. "She had not yet scrubbed those. Perchance she was about to burn them?"

"Perchance?" I said.

"Well, all we had to offer were those worn shoes in need of soles. It was a fair trade. She did throw in a pan of cornbread."

"What cornbread?" I said as I put on my white shoes. "I'm hungry. I could eat something."

"Sorry, I ate it while you slept," he replied and climbed back into the driver's seat.

"Nice," I said with disgust. "And stop saying I was sleeping, because I wasn't. I was out cold because you head-butted me."

"Yes," he said with a haughty grin. "Like a stag of the wild."

"Where I come from only pro-wrestlers do head-butts."

"Pro-wrestlers," he said with genuine appreciation. "I shall take that as the highest of compliments."

146

CHAPTER 26

On the road, we came upon a barefoot man in tattered clothes and a straw hat limping the same direction. He carried his belongings tied up in a handkerchief on the end of a stick. I was instantly reminded of Jim, the runaway slave, from *The Adventures of Huckleberry Finn.* I guessed him to be in his mid to late 20s. As we drew near, he got off the road, removed his hat and bowed his head. I noticed his left leg was twisted — either an old injury or birth defect. Virgil didn't acknowledge him. We were almost past when the man spoke.

"Suh! Beg pard'n!"

Virgil still did not acknowledge him.

"Suh? Can ya hep me?"

I waited for Virgil to reply, but he ignored the request for help. I turned to the man. "What do you need?" I asked him.

At this Virgil said to me, "Don't encourage that darky beggar."

The man put his hat back on and hopped alongside the wagon, favoring his leg and doing his best to smile. "Da name is Jacob, an' I's no beggah, suh. I's lookin' fuh woik. I's a good field hand. I knows tobaccuh, I knows cotton, I knows hemp an' sorghums. I can hep ya break ground. I woiks hard, an' I loves Jesus."

"Do I look like a farmer or a parson to you?" Virgil said. "I have no use for a gimpy, Jesus-loving field hand."

The man was undaunted. He laughed in a self deprecating way and took off his hat again. "Oh, nahsuh. Sorry, suh. Is plain ya don' need no field hand. Shoo, I's a fool tuh even think ya wud. Nahsuh, nahsuh. But I's a good stable boy too, an' I can drive a team."

"I don't need a driver. Now be off," Virgil replied then he clucked to the horse and snapped the reins to make her go faster, and the mare shifted into a trot. Jacob picked up his pace to keep up.

"I's do whateveh ya needs. I knows you's a good man, suh. I's gots fo' moufs ta feed, an' I cud shore use da woik. I's do whateveh."

Strathmore glowered at Jacob, annoyed, then slung the reins out like a whip and slapped the poor man over his head. Jacob cowed and fell behind.

"Why'd you do that?" I asked and turned in my seat. Jacob stood in the same spot where we pulled away and stared after us.

"I told you not to encourage him," Virgil said to me. "You cannot give those darkies an inch. We are on a mission. We have no time for charity."

We traveled another several minutes through small groves and grassland to the outskirts of a homestead. The road split just ahead with one branch dissecting the property and the other leading away gradually to the west. We were on a rise, and below us in the distance, were several cleared acres, a small log cabin, a log smokehouse, an outhouse, a water well, and a barn. The buildings were all well-spaced from each other. There was a line of trees behind the buildings and beyond that, another open field for either crops or pasture. Woods bordered the property to the right and left.

A gray horse grazed near the barn, a couple dozen chickens were scattered around, and there was a small fenced-in lot against the barn, which held a milk goat and kid.

Virgil stopped at the Y in the road a couple hundred yards from the house and other buildings.

"Here we are," he said and hopped out of the wagon.

I climbed down. "I don't see or hear anyone."

"I imagine that is because, by this time, Emmet is dead and Maribeth has gone with Emmet's portion of the keys. It has now been more than an hour since Maribeth vanished from us in the woods. If she arrived immediately, it would be plenty of time for her to work her ghastly skills. But I can go ahead and retrieve the keys I have hidden and hopefully find Emmet's gold."

"What about the people who own this farm? Where are they?"

"I don't see them about. It is possible they are in the back field. It is the time of year to break ground for planting, and their two plow horses are gone. The family name is Hanes. Emmet and I each gave them a gold piece to board in their barn for a few days. They have been quite hospitable and respectful of our privacy. I hope they have not come to any harm at Maribeth's hands on my account."

"Hanes," I said, remembering. "William, Charlotte, and Polly?"

"That's right," Virgil said. "Do you know them?"

"No," I replied, but I knew what would happen to them. "What is today's date?"

"The nineteenth of April, I believe. Why do you ask?"

They were the family I had read about in the newspaper at the library. They were either already dead, or they would be dead within the next day or two. I realized, too, that the man we met on the road looking for a job was the same man who would be arrested for their murders—Jacob Massey. Maribeth had given Thaddeus warnings about disrupting the timeline by changing things in the past, but I couldn't just let this family be killed. I turned to Virgil and said, "If they are still alive, we have to warn them. We have to make them leave this place for a few days—save them from the gurelach."

"There is a gurelach here?" Virgil said, alarmed.

"If not yet, there will be."

A worried expression darkened his face. "Maribeth has my astra. The pistol in my pocket is useless against the demons. We should leave this place and devise a different plan."

"Please," I said. "The Hanes family will be murdered and another man falsely accused. We have to warn them away before it happens. And we have to find Maribeth; I can't get back home without her."

Virgil gave a snort. "Maribeth has lied to you. We do not need her, only the keys. Perhaps we can thwart her on the road away from here. I suspect she will leave Kinsville by train. We might be able to catch up with her and take back the keys."

"Gurelach or no gurelach, I am going to that house to try and save that family. If you want me to help you gain asylum on my world, then you need to come along with me now. Otherwise, take your chances with Östric."

I am a horrible liar, but I hoped Virgil would buy my posturing, because I wasn't sure if I was brave enough to approach that house by myself.

He stared out at the cabin with distaste and released a reluctant sigh. "I don't know how you have foreknowledge of a murder here, but...as you wish." He reached into the hip pocket of my jeans and pulled out the little Derringer. "Arm yourself, lad. This is reckless business you're leading us into. Even with my medallion, I shall have little defense against a prolonged gurelach attack. I once witnessed an agent torn to pieces."

I walked over to a big oak tree and found a stick on the ground large enough to use as a club.

"Okay," I said. "I'm ready."

150

Virgil shook his head. "I am dubious."

We followed the wagon path down toward the structures. Being the latter part of April, the grass was a lush green, about knee high, and dotted with fuzzy, white dandelion heads.

"It's quiet," I said, feeling the need to whisper.

"Yes," Virgil whispered a reply. "I noticed. Be alert."

As we drew near, the gray horse by the barn lifted its head and whinnied. Behind us, the nag with the wagon nickered a reply. A breeze moved like a wave over the top of the grass. A door creaked on its hinges then slammed shut.

"Yonder is Emmet," Virgil said softly and indicated direction with the nod of his head. "He's alive and alone."

A tall, husky man with a thick red mustache and a cocked, maroon bowler strode on the path between the barn and the outhouse as if he didn't have a care. He stopped at the outhouse, unhitched his suspenders, and went inside. He never looked our way.

"I guess Maribeth hasn't been here yet," I said.

"Either that, or Emmet bested her."

I nodded and said, "He *is* a big dude."

"Do not call him that in his presence. He fancies himself a man of the world and has no use for dandies."

"Okay," I said, but I was confused. "What's the plan?"

Virgil let out a heavy breath. "I suppose we should shut him up in the privy until I can make a proper assessment. You hold the door shut on him while I check the barn for Maribeth and the keys."

"Why should *I* hold the door on him?" I asked, not liking the plan at all.

"I don't want Emmet angry with me. He and I made a pact, and if he thinks I reneged, he could get rather mean about it."

"Well, I don't want him angry with me either," I argued. "Maybe we could just talk to him about it."

151

"That's not Emmet's way," Virgil replied. "If it is I who restrains him, the two of us will be in trouble when he is loosed. If it is you who does the deed, I shall convince him it was a misunderstanding."

"Sounds iffy to me."

"Do you wish to save this family, or no?"

"Ugh, okay."

We jogged in a crouch toward the outhouse then closed the rest of the distance on tiptoes. The little building was narrow and built from rough planks. There was a small circle cut out high in the door to allow in light and air. I eased in and put my weight against the door.

"Who's there?" said a raspy voice from inside.

I didn't answer. Virgil gave me an apologetic wave and ran off to the barn.

"Who is there?!" The voice demanded again.

"Sorry about this," I squeaked.

"Oh, I'll make ya sorry," was the reply. I noticed a muddled Irish accent.

Emmet pushed against the door. I dug my foot into the dirt. He pushed again. Then he shook it. I stared longingly over at the barn.

"Let me out!" Emmet bellowed.

"Sorry!"

"Stop sayin' ya sorry, ya Missy! I'm ona drag me boot in ya sorry teeth."

"Please don't," I said, cringing. "It's a misunderstanding. You'll see. I promise...and my name's not Missy."

"Oooh, Missy!" he cooed through one of the cracks in between the boards. "I'm ona git outta here, I am. You can betcha knickers." Then he growled and slammed against the door. It popped open about an inch then shut again

"Misunderstanding! Misunderstanding!"

"I understand jus' fine."

"Please! What about the family that lives here? Are they safe?"

"Eh?"

"Where is the Hanes family?!" I said.

"They went into town to spend their gold," he said.

"Do you know when they'll be back?"

His reply was to blast a hole in the door near my head with a gun I didn't know he had.

"No!" I yelled. "Virgil is here! I'm with Virgil! I'm a friend!"

"Virgil?" he said. There was a long pause, and he continued. "Bugger all. That wee squart has betrayed me, hasn't he?"

"Not at all," I said. "He and I are here to—"

Another bullet blew through the door.

"Stop it!" I cried. "Östric! And gurelachs! And keys....and...." my voice dissolved into sobs.

Then Virgil appeared in the doorway of the barn. He held an ornate wooden box. There was a carving on the side of the Flower of Life.

"Is that it?" I called to him with a sniffle. "Did you find the keys?"

"I did," he said. "All except the white one. No sign of Maribeth." Then he held up a small bag. "I also found Emmet's share of the gold. Emmet, the clumsy oaf, left his astra in the barn, so I have it too."

"Virgil!" Emmet yelled.

"Is it safe to let him out now?" I asked.

Virgil squinted up into the sky as if thinking it over then he grinned. "I would not do that. You've gone and made Emmet angry. If I was you, I'd see to it he never left that privy."

"But—"

"Virgil!" Emmet roared and slammed against the door again. "As soon as I've torn the arms from this missus, I'll deal with you!"

"Best of luck to you, lad," Virgil said to me. "I now need to go to my hiding place and retrieve my own share of the earnest money then catch the next train out of Kinsville." He gave me a little salute and ran back up the path toward the wagon.

CHAPTER 27

I was helpless as Virgil Strathmore escaped to the buckboard. I was certain my way back home was in that box. I had to do something to stop him.

"Um, Mr. McCain, is it?" I said to the man in the outhouse. "If I open this door, will you promise to let me go?"

"I'll let ya go, girly," Emmet replied. Then he added, "To perdition."

"Virgil is getting away! He has the box and your share of the gold!"

Emmet kicked the door. He wasn't going to cooperate. I still held that oak limb I had grabbed for a weapon. I caught one end of my club into a knothole in the outhouse door then I shoved the other end into the dirt, wedging the door shut. With caution, I let some of my weight off the door. Emmet kicked again, but the door only budged a little. It wouldn't hold him in for long, but maybe it would keep him there long enough for me to get away and catch Virgil.

I had just started to run after him when I noticed a flicker of blue light out of the corner of my eye. I stumbled to a stop and turned around. Maribeth crouched next to the outhouse. She was transparent and wispy like a ghost. Strands of her long, blonde hair poked out of the bottom of Virgil's stolen top hat and fluttered in the breeze. She still held the white key. Five snarling gurelachs surrounded her, ready to pounce.

The body of one of the creatures had materialized partially inside the outhouse. Emmet roared, "What in blazes!?" when he discovered the demon's hind parts in there with him. He kicked harder against the door.

Maribeth saw me. "The gurelachs are coming through!" she yelled, but her voice sounded far away. She dropped the key, reached into her coat and came out with an astra in both hands.

She stood and lifted both astrae at two of the monsters on either side of her. Tendrils of blue light arced between the horns of the weapons, and the air rippled out from their ends like a shockwave. There was no noise from the weapon, but Maribeth's elbows bent with the recoil, and then blue light belched out and hammered the opposing monsters. One of the creatures caught the full force, and its body disintegrated into a splattering of black blood and meat chunks. The second demon lost an arm and flipped away like a ragdoll to fade into the oblivion from whence it came.

Maribeth stomped the crystal key with the heel of her boot. The crystal fractured. She was about to pick it up, but the other gurelachs closed in. Instead, she spun around like the needle of a compass to line up her weapons with two of the three remaining monsters, but the demons shrank back to avoid her. She and her attackers were more solid now. The one creature fully entered the little building with Emmet McCain.

The outhouse shuddered and rocked as Emmet and the gurelach tangled with each other inside. "Le' me out, blast ya!" Emmet demanded. A board from the privy's door splintered outward. Emmet's gun went off a third time.

Maribeth and the gurelachs were no longer transparent by this time; they were fully solid, fully there. One of the monsters saw me and rushed in. There was no time for me to react. Thankfully, Maribeth was faster. With a flash of blue light, the thing's naked, yellow legs vaporized in a spray of inky gore. It shrieked in pain, but continued to pull itself toward me on the ground with its talon-like fingers. Blue light flashed again, and its head exploded.

The other monster bounded away past the house toward the distant woods. Maribeth tracked its movement. Just before the thing made it to the trees, she let fly with both astrae. It and two large sycamore trees sizzled out of existence in a puff of black. Then she knelt and picked up the freshly re-broken white key. It was in two pieces. She tossed a piece to me and slipped the other into her pocket.

"If we get separated, break it again," she said. "You know what to do."

To be honest, I wasn't 100% certain what to do at all, but I nodded anyway.

She then turned toward the noisy outhouse and yelled. "Is that you in there, Emmet McCain?! You've got something that doesn't belong to you!"

"Virgil is the one you're after!" I called to her over my shoulder as I ran to chase after the wagon. "Hurry, he has the keys, and he's getting away!"

"Catch him," she commanded. "I'll be right behind you!" She ran to the gray horse by the barn.

Virgil Strathmore was turning the buckboard around to take the road back to Kinsville. Meanwhile, another figure stood on the branch of road that split away. It was the barefoot field hand, Jacob. I wondered if he had witnessed all of the recent bizarre excitement or if he had just walked up.

"Stop him!" I yelled to Jacob. "He's a thief!"

Even though Jacob was some distance away from me, his posture and body language told me he wasn't sure if he wanted to get involved. He looked from me to Virgil, but didn't move.

"Stop! Thief!" I yelled again.

Virgil snapped the reins, and the horse started. My arms and legs were pumping hard, but there would be no way I'd catch Virgil on foot once he got rolling.

Finally, either out of a desire for revenge against the man who had hit him, or for the possibility of a reward for catching a thief, or because he loved Jesus and it was the right thing to do, Jacob finally acted. Going as quickly as his bad leg would allow, he ran alongside the wagon for a few feet, and then shoved his hobo stick through the spokes of the left rear wagon wheel. The buckboard hopped, dragged along the path a few more feet then stopped when the horse gave up. Jacob vaulted over the side into the back of the wagon, and Virgil turned to face him, Derringer in hand.

Behind me were hoof beats. Just as I turned, Maribeth thundered past me at a full gallop riding bareback with a handful of mane. The top hat was gone. Her long hair and open jacket flapped behind her like battle flags.

There was a puff of smoke from the end of Virgil's Derringer, and Jacob clutched his chest. A second later came the report of the gun. Jacob crumpled into the wagon. Maribeth's mechanism came to life, and her own pistol appeared. She drew down on Virgil and fired from horseback. It was a miss. He climbed from the wagon, reached back inside for the ancient box, and made haste for the woods with the treasure tucked awkwardly under his arm. Maribeth didn't fire again due to the risk of hitting the box.

However, there was another gunshot, and it came from behind me. Emmet McCain, in that smelly and confined space, still lived and fought the remaining gurelach.

Maribeth had no trouble intercepting Virgil before he escaped into the trees. She slowed the horse just ahead of the fleeing man then slipped from her mount in a fluid, graceful move that put her right in his path and unavoidable. She lifted her astra, and Virgil responded by holding the box in front of him as a shield.

"Take care where you point that, Maribeth," he said.

I made it to the wagon by that time. The front of Jacob's shirt was red with blood and more blood trickled from the side of his mouth. He stared up into the sky and struggled to breathe.

"Jacob, can you hear me?" I asked him, but he didn't answer.

"Give me the box," Maribeth said. "You have made my life difficult long enough."

"You cannot make demands of me, woman!"

I patted Jacob's hand. "I'll get you help," I assured him.

"Ain't no heppin' dis," he said.

"You!" I shouted at Maribeth and Virgil as I strode toward them. "Stop this! I need a medallion! He's going to die!"

"Get back, boy!" Maribeth said. "I'm not stopping anything until I get what I came for."

Virgil lifted an astra of his own, and aimed it at Maribeth. The blue fingers of light danced between the horns. Just as the air rippled around it, Maribeth dodged to the side. The shot missed her and burned out the midsection of the tree behind her. The top of the tree dropped with a crash, and Maribeth had to scramble away again to keep from being crushed by it.

Virgil shifted his attention away from Maribeth and pointed the astra at me instead.

"Lad, I don't wish any animosity betwixt myself and you're employers, but I will shoot you if you come closer."

I stopped then pointed back to the wagon. "That man will die unless you heal him!"

"He is no one of consequence," he said with a shrug. "Now, run along and catch that gray horse for me. I must take my leave."

"No," I said. "I'm not going to help you."

"Then I bid you farewell."

His astra came to life once more. The points of the weapon glowed. There was nowhere I could go. I lifted my arm in front of my face in a vain attempt to defend myself. Then, Maribeth charged in. Virgil's astra discharged just as she tackled him, but his aim was off. The blast of blue energy gouged a hole in the ground in front of me, and I was tossed backward in a shower of turf.

Dazed, I sat up and rubbed the grit from my eyes. I was met with flickering color. I rubbed my eyes again; I wasn't sure what I was seeing. It was like a laser light show. The box lay on the ground on its side, and the lid was open. The colorful crystal keys had spilled out in a pile. Some of them were broken. Energy, like lightning, of every color in the rainbow arced and sparked and skittered upright along the ground within a tight area around the box. Virgil and Maribeth wrestled in the middle of it all. They rolled and grunted, hands around each others' throat.

Something else was happening. The air around the box, the agents, and the dancing lights was distorted. It reminded me of the effect of heat rising from pavement. Maribeth and Virgil were oblivious and only interested in killing each other. I was reluctant to trust either of them, but if I was going to save Jacob and make it back to my time, my best option was to help Maribeth.

I took a step forward, and that's when the gateway opened.

CHAPTER 28

White light flashed in the midst of the distortion just above the two fighting agents. I blinked away the spots, and I saw a perfect iridescent ring of light big enough to drive a bus through. Inside that ring was a different place. There was a meadow of yellow grass and several tall, stone monuments. Wind howled out of the opening carrying with it a scent that was vaguely familiar, like cloves and peppercorns.

Virgil and Maribeth stopped fighting to gaze in awe through the portal. Around and through them, the colorful light show continued to dance and spark. There was another flash of white light, and the scene in the window changed to darkness illuminated from below by a lake of fiery lava. I felt the heat of it. I smelled the smoke and sulfur.

"Dear God!" Virgil cried.

Another flash changed the scene to the sea and the smell to salt and fish. It changed again to show a modern, albeit alien, city. With each change of scene the wind increased until it reached near hurricane strength.

"We have to secure the keys!" Maribeth yelled. "Put them back in the box!"

The two of them, on hands and knees, snatched up the crystal pieces along with handfuls of grass and dirt and tried to shove them back into their slots in the box. When keys of different colors touched each other, another arc of energy would shoot into the air.

The scene changed again, and I gasped. It was me in there. I was in an empty space with Thaddeus, Lacy, and scores of gurelachs. I caught a whiff of ammonia. It was the event that had happened in my living room the day before.

Then the wind made an alarming change. At first, it rushed out to us, filling our nostrils with the odors of the other worlds, but the direction shifted. Now it tugged at me. Maribeth and Virgil felt it too.

The two worked harder to collect the strewn and broken crystals and return them to their homes. The pull of the vacuum grew stronger. I smelled ozone and burned hair. The scenes in the window changed faster while the roar of the wind grew louder. The horses bucked and reared, and the buckboard tipped over and Jacob tumbled out. The old mare, still harnessed, fell with it, but was able to stand again and run away when the wagon's hitch shaft broke.

The scenes in the portal now shifted at least once per second. Maribeth's legs lifted off the ground. She screamed and clutched the grass.

"Maribeth!" Virgil and I yelled at the same time. The world through the gateway was dark and stormy. Purple lightning etched the sky and illuminated a craggy cliff face. The grass on our side of the portal, Maribeth's last anchor to this Earth, pulled out by the roots, and she was sucked away into the darkness. The scene changed again—sunny slopes and grazing animals.

Virgil turned to me, his eyes wide with fear. "You have to help me shut it, lad!"

He lay on his belly, scraped up the remaining crystals, and hugged them up close.

"Lad?!" he pleaded. It dragged him backwards. He rolled to his back and tried to stop his movement with his heels. One last scream, and he slipped inside. He had managed to hold onto the keys, but he could not keep the box; it was still there on the ground. The shimmering, shifting gateway shrank to nothing leaving only a pinpoint of light which shone for a few seconds about three feet off the ground then faded.

It was over. The world appeared normal again, but I knew it wasn't. I still remained in 1877, and the box belonging to the Nepheel was still there too. Hesitantly, I walked over to the spot where Virgil Strathmore and Maribeth had been yanked away. I picked up the box. Inside, there was a shallow false bottom, and there was another raised carving of the Flower of Life. In each circle of the flower there were holes for each of the keys. Each hole was identified by a specific colored symbol. They went in order of the color wheel—red, orange, yellow, green, blue, and violet. In the middle, rather than the center ring having one hole, it had two—a space for a white crystal and another for a black crystal. I supposed that each circle represented one of the worlds, but there were only seven— eight if the holes for the crystal keys were counted rather than the circles. Evidently, not all of the worlds were represented.

Before they were pulled through the gate, Maribeth and Virgil had managed to replace the blue key (shoved into the yellow hole) and broken pieces of the yellow and violet keys were loose in the top. I found a piece of the red in the grass nearby. The rest of the crystals and pieces had been sucked away with the agents.

There was evidence all around of our visit to this time—the felled and vaporized trees, stolen and traded goods, and I had interacted with four different people from this period. And what about Virgil and Maribeth? Did their disappearance happen in the original 1877? Would my timeline be changed? I had no idea if any of these things would negatively affect the timeline of my world.

There was nothing I could do about any of that anyway. I couldn't worry about the future right then; I had to focus on the immediate—the dying man behind me. I ran back to the overturned wagon to check on Jacob.

"Jacob?" I said as I knelt beside him. He was in the same position which the wagon had dumped him—on his side with one arm over his head. Not far away, scattered next to the wagon were several gold coins. It was Virgil's and Emmet's earnest money. I rolled Jacob to his back and checked for breathing. It was faint.

I was unsure how to help him. Maribeth and Virgil had taken their medallions with them. Maybe if Lacy had been there, her limited medical knowledge would have helped, but it was just me, and I'd never even taken a first aid class. Then I remembered Emmet McCain.

"He's an agent too," I said. "He should have a medallion."

When I stood to run, I was able to get a clear view of the property. The outhouse was on its side. All that remained on the original spot was a square wooden base and a squatting platform. The rest of the building was a shambles. Emmet's feet were sticking out of a hole in the broken structure, but there was no sign of the gurelach he'd been fighting. There was a high possibility I'd have to confront one of the two in order to get that medallion, but I went anyway.

When I arrived, I paused before looking inside to do a quick scan of my surroundings in an attempt to locate the gurelach. I neither saw it, nor any trail or tracks to indicate the direction it had gone. I feared it had escaped to the woods and would likely be the creature that would kill the Hanes family.

Once I was sure the monster was not nearby, I bent down and peered into the shadows of the wrecked outhouse. The first thing I noticed, other than the smell of urine and feces, was the medallion's blue glow. It was attempting to heal Emmet's wounds, which at that moment were difficult to discern in the low light. I got up and opened the outhouse door like the top of a chest. The sight made me gag and retch.

Emmet's left arm, still clutching a revolver, was torn from his body and lay up near his head. His belly was ripped open from sternum to groin. Yet he still hung on to life. His chest rose and fell with strangled breaths. I wasn't sure if the medallion could mend him; the damage was so severe. I was just standing there debating with myself whether it would be ethical to take it from him to save Jacob when the blue light dimmed and went dark. He was dead.

I didn't know the man, but I had not liked him very much. He might not have been as old as Maribeth, but he was one of the agents of the Nepheel, so he had lived a long and interesting life. I felt no sorrow at his passing. I leaned over into the outhouse (now very much like a coffin) and lifted the medallion over his head. His lifeless eyes seemed to give me an accusing stare.

"Sorry," I said, "but I need this more than you." Then I pried the revolver out of his hand. "I might need this too."

Jacob was fading when I returned.

"You're going to be okay," I said, out of breath from my run. "Just hang on."

I quickly put the medallion around his neck and positioned it near the bullet wound. The blue crystal in the center lit up again. I noticed a positive change in Jacob's breathing right away. I was optimistic, but I anticipated it might take a while since his injury was much like Virgil's had been.

I tried to make him comfortable then I said, "I'll be back to check on you in a few minutes."

CHAPTER 29

I counted the gold pieces as I dropped them back into the leather drawstring bag. There were twenty-nine coins of different denominations with a collective face value of close to $300. In my own time in the future, these coins probably would be worth a fortune. If I was unable to return to that time, I would, at least, have some money to live on for a while. Emmet McCain and Virgil Strathmore certainly would not need it anymore.

After ensuring the health and safety of Jacob and the Hanes family, and planting a piece of the crystal at the gristmill, my first purchase would be some food; I hadn't eaten since breakfast...one hundred and thirty something years from now. I would also need clothes; new would be preferable and clean would be a must. I'd probably need to purchase a bath too. I tightened the string on the bag and put it with the Nepheel's Flower of Life box next to the stump of the tree Virgil had destroyed.

I held up the broken piece of white key. Maribeth said to break it again if we were separated. I wasn't sure what she meant when she told me that, but I now understood. I needed to break it again and keep a piece with me. Another piece had to be hidden in the gristmill where it could be activated by the lightning during the storm in my future. I didn't know how long it would take to pull me back after I put it in the mill. It might work instantly, or it might take years. Hopefully, it would rescue Maribeth too. There was a possibility it might get activated by the storm on her end, and take me to whatever place she'd been dragged, which I didn't want. I had to get to the gristmill as soon as I was sure Jacob was well enough for me to leave him.

I put the white key into its place inside the box. Then I went back to check on Jacob. I was happy to find him coming around. He blinked at me and sat up.

"Hold on," I said before he could bolt. "How do you feel?"

"He shot me," he said. Then he saw his bloody shirt and panicked. "Oh, lawd! Blood!" He cried.

"No, it's okay. You'll be okay!"

He lifted the glowing medallion away from his chest with wide eyes, "A witch's charm! I won't have nuffin' to do wif no witch!" He tried to yank it off but I stopped him.

"No," I said. "It's not magic. I promise it is good." Then on impulse I added, "God sent me to heal you."

He froze and cut his eyes at me, skeptical.

"This medallion will heal you," I continued. "It gives long life and healing. Your wound is probably already gone. See for yourself."

He wasn't sure if he could trust me. Cautiously, he lifted his shirt. There was drying blood on his chest and stomach, but the bullet hole was gone. The bullet itself was loose inside his shirt and dropped to the ground. For some reason, the medallion continued to glow. Perhaps it was working on his deformed leg.

"When the blue light goes dark, it means your healing is finished," I said. "Keep it on until then."

He stared at the medallion a moment then smiled up at me. "You's a angel."

"No," I said. "I'm just a...helper. Maybe you could help me. I know you're looking for work. I want to hire you. We'll need some clothes and food, and I have to go to the gristmill. There's a body down there and—"

"Git you clothes and food? I know dat from da good book. I's entertainin' Jesus unawares! I shudda knowed it wiff dose perty white shoes." He smiled and waved me off. "Shoo, Jesus, you ain't gotta pay me nuffin."

"No, really, I'm not Jesus or an angel or—"

He yelped in surprise and hopped to his feet. "A devil!"

"What?! No, I'm not a devil either!"

"Naw! A devil!" he pointed past me. "A devil!"

I stood and turned. He was right. There was a devil by the barn. The gurelach that killed Emmet had returned. It was stalking the chickens. This was my opportunity to kill the thing before it could harm the Hanes family. I pulled Emmet's Colt revolver from my waistband. I couldn't remember how many times he had fired, but I thought I still had two shots left. This weapon could kill the monster; I had witnessed Thaddeus do it in the museum, but I would need to be close to it to ensure I didn't miss. My hands trembled just considering it. I wasn't sure I could go through with it. What if I failed? What if I died? I didn't want to wind up like Emmet or Carl or the poor guy attacked in front of the drug store, but if I didn't try, the Hanes family would die and Jacob would take the fall for it.

I turned again to Jacob, but he had gone to hide behind the overturned wagon.

"I'm going to try to kill it," I said and hoped he might volunteer to help me.

Instead, he cowered even more behind the wagon. "Mind ya'seff, Jesus!"

"I'm not Jesus," I said. "My name is Robert, Robert Bright. I'm just a kid, for crying out loud!"

That last part was an attempt to shame him into coming along, but it didn't work. Jacob's head sank more so that only his eyes peeked up over the side, and he sang, *"Rock of ages, clef' fo' me, le' me hide mysef in deee."*

"Okay," I said and set off to face the gurelach.

"Let da wahtuh an' da bloood..." At this point, his song changed from singing to humming.

Ahead, the gurelach ran along on all fours darting after a particular buff-colored chicken, nipping at the bird's tail feathers with its saw blade teeth. The monster's naked, yellow skin was speckled red with Emmet's blood.

My legs felt rubbery. I patted my gun, hoping to gain a little courage, but instead I found my mind on my dad and his insistence on having appreciation for historical items. I held in my hand an early first generation Colt Single Action Army — The Peacemaker — "the gun that won the west". We had the rusty remains of one just like this in the museum. It had been unearthed in Kinsville in the 1970s when they were digging a foundation for a new shopping center. For that matter, it could have been this very gun. A weapon like this, in this condition, would bring a few thousand dollars at auction in my time.

There I was trudging down to what could possibly be my own messy demise, and I was hearing my dad's instruction to *"put on the white gloves, Robbie, or the oil from your fingers will damage the patina."*

I sighed. I would have felt a whole lot better if I could have used an astra.

About halfway there, Jacob stopped humming long enough to shout, "Give 'em hell, Jesus!" The gurelach heard him. It perked up and stared directly at me. At first, it regarded me with a curious gesture like a dog cocking its head to one side.

"Nice boy," I said in a shaky voice.

Its bloody lips spread into a menacing smile. A feather dangled from between its teeth.

"That's a good boy," I said. "Nice boy."

It opened its impossibly large mouth and made a vocalization like something from a dinosaur movie. When it stood erect, it was almost a man, yet it was not a man in so many frightening ways.

"I have something for you," I said.

It didn't come at me the way I expected. Instead, it hunched and began to pace like a caged animal. I got to within twenty feet of it and stopped. Surely I could hit it from this distance. I lifted the revolver and held it as steady as my shaking hands would allow. The creature stopped pacing and glared at me. I closed one eye and sighted down the barrel at my target. My thumb found the rough surface of the hammer and cocked it back—click, click, click.

Then the gurelach spoke! It was a raspy whisper, but it did speak; I was sure of it.

I opened both eyes and took my attention away from the gun sights.

"Say what?"

It repeated it for me. "Baaahh-haaalll." The word or words were a gurgling hiss, but it was language.

We stared at each other for a couple of seconds then I snapped out of it and squeezed the trigger. The end of The Peacemaker bounced with the recoil, and the demon twirled. I winged it. It made the dinosaur sound again and bounded away toward the woods.

"No!" I yelled and cocked the hammer again. "Come back!" I sighted up with the beast and pulled the trigger a second time, but nothing happened. I tried again, but the monster had escaped. I pushed the Colt into the front of my pants and pulled my shirt over it.

My hesitance and fear had kept me from going in close to make the kill. I had let it get away, and now the Hanes family was in danger again. Back up the path by the overturned wagon, Jacob stood and gave me a big wave. Jacob was once again in danger of losing his life too…to a lynch mob's noose.

CHAPTER 30

It was a big possibility that I would not be able to change the past. It was possible that fate was real and William, Charlotte, and Polly Hanes would be killed by the gurelach no matter how much I tried to stop it.

I walked back up the path, picked up the bag of gold and went to join Jacob at the buckboard. He came out to meet me halfway. His limp was less pronounced, but he didn't mention it. The medallion around his neck still glowed. It was taking a while to heal his leg. There was also a chance that there were other things wrong—maybe a tumor or an illness that wouldn't become known for a few years.

"I just want to be certain," I said, "Your name is Jacob Massey. Is that right?"

"Yeah suh," he nodded.

"Let's sit," I said. He sat cross-legged at my feet, eyes fixed, like a dutiful disciple of Jesus. I sat across from him with the bag of gold next to me. I paused to consider how much I should tell him.

"The devil will return," I said. "When it does, it will kill the family who lives on this farm. Their deaths will be blamed on you."

He looked down the hill at the cabin then turned to me. "I ain't killed nobody," he said. "I swear."

"I know," I said.

"But dey'll hang me iffin dey thinks I do."

"That's what we need to prevent," I said. "Mr. Hanes and his family must be warned to stay away from here for a few days. Can I hire you to do a job for me?"

He gave me a vigorous nod.

I opened the bag of gold and pulled out two $5 coins. I didn't know what that much money could buy in 1877, but Jacob's face lit up when he saw the money.

"I have to go into town to the mill right away. Otherwise, I might get stuck here. There's a dead man in the outhouse. That devil killed him. His body has to be disposed of."

"Dead man? Lawd, devil get me hanged fo' sho'."

"If I pay you this gold, would you please get rid of the body and the outhouse?"

Jacob balked when I mentioned what the job would be, so I pulled out two $20 coins. "You'll get these when the job is done. You don't have to dig a hole. Just pull him out into the woods some distance and roll him into a creek or something. It's not ideal, but he needs to be away from here so no one can find him or connect him to this place...or to you." Then I added. "Plus you can keep whatever gold or other personal items you find on the man. He has no family, so don't think of it as stealing."

He thought it over then agreed and took the $5 coins.

"Use one of the horses, if you can catch them," I said. "And try to stay out of sight. If anyone sees you in those bloody clothes, they'll suspect you of something even if they don't find the body. I'll buy you some new clothes when I'm in town. I'll be back as soon as I can." I stood and he stood with me. I pointed down the road to the west. "Do you see that big dead tree—the one that's split at the top? When you get done, you can hide there and wait for me. I'll be back as soon as I can with new clothes and the rest of your pay. If the Hanes family returns while I am away, do your best to scare them off without getting yourself shot."

I picked up the box and the bag of gold.

"If I see them on the road, I'll convince them to go back to Kinsville."

"You promise you is comin' back?"

"Yes, and I am going to want that medallion back when I do."

Jacob took the road down the hill to the homestead with barely a limp, and I turned to go back to Kinsville. Even if I could have caught one of the horses, neither one of them had a saddle or bridle, and me not being a horseman by any stretch, I doubted I'd be able to get them to go where I wanted. It would be faster if I just ran back to town. It was only about four miles. I did a 5K with Lacy once, which is just over three miles. I saw no reason why I couldn't do it again.

However, I soon realized something: gold is heavy. I had to stop while still within eyeshot of the homestead, get off the road, and hide the bag in the bushes. I pulled out five gold coins—$45 worth—and put those in my pocket to purchase some clothes and food for Jacob and me. I would have to retrieve the bag of gold later. Even though the box was just bulky enough to be cumbersome, it was too dangerous for it to be left behind, so I carried it with me.

It took me close to an hour to return to Kinsville. I jogged and ran as much as possible, but I couldn't maintain that pace consistently with the box in my arms and with less than ideal terrain. The sun was low in the sky. I would not make it back to the Hanes homestead before dark, and since there had not been anyone else on the road, I hoped the family might have decided to spend the night in town.

Most of the shops had closed for the day, so I was not able to make my purchases. I would have to get clothes for Jacob some other way. But I was pleased to find the gristmill closed as well. The whole way back to Kinsville, I had been trying to figure out how I would plant the crystal in there without being noticed by the mill's employees, but by arriving so late in the day, I had been fortunate to avoid them. Only one worker remained, and it was a stable boy putting the horses up for the night. I hid in the shadows next to a church across the road and watched the stable for several minutes to make sure he would not go back into the mill itself. When I was satisfied he would not, I ran across the dirt road to the mill. I was able to enter the unlocked door unnoticed.

I wished I still had my phone so I could have taken a picture of the inside of the place for my dad. The layout was pretty much the same as the museum. The area where my dad's office would one day be was stacked with bagged grain. The large millstone was right where it should have been in what would one day become the main gallery. The shaft and hopper and apparatus for the horses did not exist in my time, but they were all there now. In this time, the main gallery area had a roof but lacked walls and was open to the outside. Only the shop and storage rooms were enclosed.

I had to stash the crystal somewhere where it would not be found or disturbed until lightning could strike the window frames in the future. Near the millstone would be out, because I knew the stone had been moved to pour the concrete floor when the building became a museum. Plus, I didn't want to risk any damage to the key while the stone was grinding. I considered burying it right outside against the foundation wall.

Finally, I decided to hide it in the wall itself. The structure was built with a double brick wall. All I would have to do was to remove a brick and drop the crystal inside. The light was fading, so I had to work quickly. If I put it near the windows it would be closest to the power source there. I found a brick a little higher than eye level around which the mortar was loose. Then I took a small knife from a workbench, and chiseled around it more until the brick would come out. It scraped out of the hole. I reached inside hoping to find a ledge or outcropping between the walls where I could place the key to keep it from falling all the way to the ground. There was nothing, so I came up with a new plan and returned to the workbench.

I put the crystal on the floor and tapped it hard with a hammer so it fractured into two pieces. One piece was for the wall the other went into my pocket. When I put my hand into my pocket, my fingers brushed the coins, and I got a brilliant idea.

"Dad," I said with a grin, "you won't have to beg for funding for a while."

There were some empty burlap bags near the bench. I took one and spread it flat on the bench then put a piece of the key in the middle along with the five gold coins. Then there was another flash of brilliance. I lifted my shirt and pulled Emmet McCain's Colt from my pants. I placed it with the other items and wrapped it all up in the burlap.

The gun was long enough that I was able to wedge the package between the two walls without it dropping. I situated it to the left of the hole as far as I could reach then replaced the brick.

"Four bricks to the right of the window's right center pane," I said so I would remember.

After brushing away the mortar dust from the floor, I picked up the box and headed for the door.

It was dusk.

When I got outside, the box started to warm up in my arms. The rings that formed the symbol of The Flower of Life were glowing. It was yellow at first, but then it went to orange then red then everything everywhere was brilliant blue light.

CHAPTER 31

I was on the front porch of the gristmill, only now it was the museum again. The sun was high in the sky, it was warm outside, and the traffic that moved on 5th Street was cars, not horses. I had returned. The box in my hands was cool and no longer emitted light.

I peeked through the window in the door then cautiously went inside. The ladder was still propped up. There were shattered bricks on the floor from the hole Maribeth had made when she removed Thaddeus' astra from the wall. I must not have been gone long.

There were agitated voices.

"Hello?" I said.

The voices stopped and Lacy came around the corner from the main gallery. Her pant leg was still stained with blood from the bullet wound, now healed.

"You're back!" she yelled, ran toward me, and hugged me over the box. "We've been worried." Then she pulled away and frowned at my clothes. "What are you wearing? You stink."

"How long have I been gone?" I asked.

"Almost two hours," she said. "Did that awful woman come back with you?"

"Maribeth? No."

"Good," she said.

"She's really not that bad once you—"

"Where have you been?" demanded another voice. I looked up to see Edith Haber, hands on hips, standing in the main gallery. She was pale and plump with a scowl and a helmet of blue rinse hair. Thaddeus stepped into view behind her and gave me a hesitant wave.

"How long has she been here?" I asked Lacy in a low voice.

"Long enough for me to learn to hate her," Lacy whispered her reply.

"Hate is a strong word," I said. "But I totally understand."

"I asked you a question!" Edith said.

"Out," I replied. "I've been out."

"So you just left the building unattended and went out? That's not a very professional way to run things. This organization uses city funds, you know. I found these two in here alone. They could have robbed the place. The hippy looking man wasn't even dressed, so I can only imagine what they must have been up to in here. The city doesn't pay you to go out."

"You don't pay me at all," I said. "Besides, we're closed for repairs."

"What repairs? I don't see any repairmen around, but I do see a mess. I do see extensive damage to this historical building. This building is owned by the city, in case you forgot."

"Right," I said. "Well we have to talk to the insurance company first, and Carl used to do a lot of our repairs and…and…and what exactly can I do for you, Ms. Haber? I've had a very long, rough day."

"I'll tell you what you can do for me. You and your father can answer my phone calls for one," she said. "For another, you can keep me informed about what goes on here. If you're going to squander taxpayer money, you should at least account

177

for yourself. There was a murder in here! Did you call and discuss it with the mayor at all?"

"No, why would I? Besides, I've kind of had a lot going on, as you can imagine."

She entered the gift shop and stopped next to Lacy. "You're father has been lax. He's going to hear about it; I assure you. The museum board will hear about all of this too, and if he loses his job over all of this, there will be no one to blame but yourself. All of this reflects badly on this town."

Lacy noticed the anger building on my face and stepped between us

"Edith," she said, "I only just met you, but I think *you* reflect badly on this town. You might not realize it, but Rob and I are old enough to vote now."

Edith smiled smugly, "Kids like you are usually too lazy to make it to the polls, and I can hardly be concerned about two measly votes."

"Okay," Lacy said. "We probably lack the votes to get you out of office, but a shriveled old crone like yourself can't live forever, can you?"

Edith's mouth snapped shut, and she cocked her head to the side. For a second there, she looked like a gurelach. "I'm calling a special council meeting," she said curtly. "I'm calling in the museum board too. You can count on that."

"You can count on this," Lacy lifted the back of her fist in front of Edith's face then slowly extended her middle finger.

"Lacy, no," I said and pulled her arm down. "That's not helping."

Edith turned back toward the main gallery. "Mr. Bright, you and your friends vacate the premises, because if I have my way, your dad will no longer be employed here by tomorrow." She stormed past Thaddeus and disappeared around the corner. She took a few steps then shrieked in surprise.

Thaddeus had a view of the gallery, so I looked to him for a reaction to what he saw. When he dropped into a crouch and drew his astra, I knew it was bad.

"I don't have a clear shot!" said a woman's voice from the gallery. It was Maribeth!

"Nor I!" Thaddeus shouted.

Edith Haber screeched again. This time it was not in surprise, but pain. I brushed past Lacy so I could get to the gallery, and Thaddeus held up a hand to stop me.

"Do something!" I said. "What's happening?"

The tips of Thaddeus' astra glowed and the air around the weapon rippled. There was a flash of blue, another cry and a splatter. I started forward again, but Thaddeus blocked my way.

"You don't want to see," he said.

"There are two of them!" Maribeth yelled. "It's coming your way!"

Thaddeus let a blast fly, and pieces of the ceiling crashed down in the main gallery. The creature skittered upside down along the ceiling and entered the gift shop. I had déjà vu when the thing tilted its head back to look at me. Unlike the last time, however, I wasn't saved by a shot from Thaddeus' revolver. The monster sprang away from the ceiling and knocked me off my feet. I expected its jagged teeth to sink into me at any second. It was right there. I was at its mercy. Its broad mouth spread over my face. All I could see were teeth.

It whispered, "Bahal. Bahal," and leapt away again.

"It has the box! It took the keys!"

The creature jumped to the wall in the corner then scrambled back up to the ceiling. Thaddeus lifted his astra once more.

"No!" yelled Maribeth. "You might hit the box!"

"Better than let the demons have it!"

Thaddeus fired, and the entire lower half of the gurelach from the ribcage down turned to mush and sprayed all over the

179

wall and gift shop display. The top of the monster, still holding the box, fell and hit the floor with a splat.

"As I said before," Maribeth shoved past Thaddeus, "you're reckless."

"I swore an oath, Maribeth," Thaddeus replied. "I aim to keep it."

Maribeth was dressed much differently than the last time I saw her. She wore a black uniform with a red emblem on the left thigh and left shoulder. There was a weapon holstered on her hip I didn't recognize. Her black helmet bore the same emblem. She removed it, and we were all surprised by her new buzz haircut.

She opened the box and looked inside.

"This is all there is?" she asked me. "What did you do with the rest of the keys?"

I shrugged. "Nothing. Virgil grabbed some before he was pulled through."

"Where did he go?" she asked.

"I don't know. He was sucked in right after you were. Where did you go?"

"I had to spend the past nine months on one of the Gradi worlds fighting in a civil war," she said. "It took you long enough to do what I told you."

"But I went right away," I said. "I put the crystal here in the mill that same day, and I was immediately pulled back. I've only been back a few minutes actually."

"Hmph," she said and closed the box. "Evidently, there's a lot we don't understand about time travel and movement between worlds. I'm sure the keys being broken have complicated things further." She picked up the box. "I have to return this to Östric. He's not going to be pleased with its condition." She turned to Thaddeus, "Come along. I'll call Östric and explain things before we arrive. I know it was Emmet and Virgil who betrayed him."

"Whoa!" I said and lifted both hands. "Whoa. Stop, stop, everybody stop! You two aren't leaving yet. Look at this place! There is gurelach blood everywhere in here. I haven't gone into the other room, but...is...is Edith dead?"

"Sorry," Thaddeus said. "The demon just popped in on top of her. We tried to get a clean shot before it killed her, but we couldn't."

Lacy gasped and started to cry.

I said, "I realize you two are both agents of the Nepheel, and you're used to seeing and doing bizarre stuff and all, but surely you're not so out of touch with the real world that you don't know what a huge problem this is for me." My eyes bounced back and forth between their blank faces. "You do realize this is a problem for me, right? Right?!"

"Östric has a crew that handles things like this," Maribeth said flippantly. "I'll call them in."

"Handles things like this how?" I asked.

"They'll make all this right—clean it up."

"But Edith—"

"Edith too," Maribeth replied.

Lacy buried her head against my chest. "I was so horrible to her," she sobbed.

"What about Edith's family?" I asked Maribeth as I gently patted Lacy's back. "What do I tell them? Her car is parked outside. And how is it going to look when the police find out there have been two violent deaths in here?"

"They won't find out," Maribeth replied. "Östric's crew is good. The body, if it is ever found at all, will be made to look like an accident. As far as the gurelach mess, it will be cleaned. These knick knacks in here can all be replaced. The structural damage will be handled by your insurance, will it not? It will be fine."

She stepped over to me and extended her hand. "I'll have that white key back now."

I nodded and pulled the piece from my pocket.

181

"And the rest of it?" she said.

"Hold on," I said. "I'll get it."

I gently pushed Lacy away and went to the front window. She moved to cry on Thaddeus's shoulder. He acted a little awkward about it, but held her anyway.

I counted the bricks until I found the correct one. There was a moment of panic when I noticed the brick had been repointed with new mortar since I removed it. What if someone had already discovered the gold?

"What's the problem?" Maribeth asked.

"Hopefully nothing," I said. "I need to get some tools. I'll be right back."

I went to the storage closet, and got a hammer and screwdriver from the little toolbox my dad kept at the museum. Then I returned and chiseled the mortar from around the brick. After I slid the brick out of its place, I reached into the hole. It was still there exactly where I'd left it a few minutes, or rather decades, before.

The burlap package was covered with dust and cobwebs, and it smelled musty. I spread it out on the floor and smiled; the contents were in pristine condition. I picked up the piece of crystal and gave it to Maribeth. She smirked at the other items but didn't comment.

"I don't understand why I was brought back to today," I said. "Why didn't I return during the storm?"

"I wouldn't know," she said.

"So has that package been inside the wall this whole time? Did I always go back and do this?"

"I can't answer your questions."

"Can't or won't?"

She gave me a quick patronizing smile. "The cleaners should be here by tonight," she said as she put the crystal into the box. "You and the girl should leave and let them do their job."

"So that's it?" I said.

"What more did you expect?"

"I don't know," I said, grasping. "There is still at least one gurelach loose in town. What about that?"

"Agents will neutralize it," she said. "That's part of the job." She looked at Thaddeus and shook her head. "But it won't be us. Thaddeus is not familiar with this time, and must be acclimated to the modern world. He'll need weeks, maybe even months, of additional training. Besides, we both need to report to Östric."

"More agents will be coming to Kinsville? Will they want to talk to me?"

"No. Why would they want to talk to you?"

"I could help them. I know stuff now."

She let out a derisive laugh. "Once the cleaners are finished, dear, you're boring life will return to normal. It's back to high school pep rallies and prom dates for you. The stuff you think you know will only get you into trouble if you talk about it. That antique gun and gold should more than make up for any inconvenience of the past few days. You may also consider it payment for your silence. Trust me; you don't want to know how we pay the blabbermouths."

CHAPTER 32

Maribeth and Thaddeus left without much of a goodbye. I wasn't sure how I felt about that. On one hand, I was either scared or stressed most of the time they were in my life; on the other hand, how would I be able to just go about my regular day-to-day knowing what I knew…and knowing there was more to know?

I wrapped up the gun and gold to take home with me. Lacy and I left via the front door to avoid seeing the gruesome scene the agents had left in the main gallery. We walked around the building to the back parking lot where we'd left our cars.

"Will you make it home before your parents do?" I asked. "I'm sure those bloody jeans will generate a lot of questions."

"Yeah, they won't see me like this." She reached into her back pocket and came back with a folded stack of bills. "This is the change that was left from the money she gave me to buy Thad some clothes."

"Wow. It looks like you came out ahead on that deal." I said, trying to be jovial.

"I'm not really in the mood to joke around," she said. "Here, you take it."

"No way," I said. "After what you've been through? I think you deserve some compensation."

"There's like two thousand dollars here," she said. "I couldn't."

I pushed her hand back. "You earned it," I said. "Put it toward what you're saving for school."

"I don't even know what to do anymore," she said. She looked over at the building and started to cry again. "God, I was so mean to that old lady. I basically told her I wished she was dead, and then she was killed. This money feels dirty to me. Everything feels wrong."

"I understand what you are feeling, but your reaction to her in there was justified. She wasn't a nice person. She would have probably acted differently too if she knew it was her last day. You had no idea she was about to die, and there was nothing you could have done about it."

"It's not just that," she said. "After what Thad told me, and after what I have seen, everything feels different now."

I couldn't quit looking at her. She was disheveled and upset, but she was so beautiful to me. I was overcome with emotions for her in that moment. There was wholesomeness to this thing I felt for Lacy. It was more than just a crush, more than physical attraction. I loved her; I was sure of it. I wanted to hold her, protect her. I had secretly loved her for years but had always lacked the courage to fully express it. And now, this strong, young woman who had always mothered me and been there for me looked so vulnerable.

I clumsily pulled her in and kissed her. Her lips were warm and soft. There was the saltiness of her tears. I could have stood there like that forever. It was perfect. It felt right.

She pushed me away and gave me a look of confusion and betrayal.

"Lacy, I don't know what to say," I stammered.

She pressed the wad of cash into my hand. "I don't want this. You can keep it or give it to your dad or donate it somewhere—I don't care." Then she turned and walked to her car.

"I'll call you later," I called out to her.

She stopped and turned to face me. "Let me call you when I'm ready," she said. "I need some time, some space...at least for a while."

Softly, I said, "Whatever you want"

She got into her car, and left.

The next few days were a numb blur. As promised by Maribeth, the Old Mill Museum was spick-and-span by the next morning. I never saw a crew arrive, and I never saw them leave, but they came just the same. There were no more reports of chimpanzees or other strange creatures in town.

My dad returned two days after the agents' departure just as depressed and lacking in funds as when he had left. His trip had been a total failure. He and I were questioned by the police as to the whereabouts of Edith Haber, then later that evening, Edith's car and remains were discovered on the railroad tracks twenty miles away—the unfortunate victim of a fiery collision. It was ruled an accident.

Östric's people were indeed good at their jobs.

Dad dealt with the insurance people and arrangements were made to repair the building. With each new thing, my dad bowed more under the pressure, and each day was packed with stress. I had not yet told him about the gold or the antique gun, because I wanted to be sure he wanted to stay. I wanted his decision to be based on his own passion for his work and not because of money. If he stayed on as the director of the museum, I knew he would use all the proceeds from any sale of the items I brought back to fund the museum. If he decided to leave, the gold would make a nice contribution to his retirement fund, or at least help him stay on his feet. After all, those items were mine to dole out as I saw fit.

The day after dad's return, we attended the funeral for Carl, the museum's handyman. My dad was as gracious as ever. I watched him from the other side of the room as he

186

consoled Carl's family, knowing that he was grieving himself at his own failure to secure funding for the museum, and I knew I'd never be the man he was. There was no question why he was chosen to be one of Carl's pallbearers.

During this whole time, with the failures and the interrogation and the pressure, I never received any messages from Lacy. I had always received messages from Lacy, whether E-mails or phone calls or texts—always, from the time we were in elementary school. I had no idea how lonely her silence would make me feel.

At Carl's graveside services, I stood about three back from the casket, and I was pondering whether my initial decision concerning the gold and my dad was right. Perhaps I should just give up the gold and gun so dad could decide for himself. I was pondering these things, when a man stepped behind me and whispered in my ear.

"Robert Bright," he said. "Don't look at me, just nod if you hear and understand me."

I felt a jolt of excitement which could have been interpreted as fear, but I didn't dare turn my head. Moving only my eyes, I scanned the crowd around me to see if anyone else noticed this man talking to me. The minister continued to speak at the head of the grave, and the other people around me either kept their eyes fixed on the speaker or on the ground.

"Do you understand?" the man whispered again.

I nodded the affirmative.

"We need to talk," he said.

I nodded again that I understood.

"Meet me by the tree at the edge of the cemetery," he said. "The dead one that's split at the top."

There was something so familiar about that. I turned around—I couldn't help it—but he was gone.

187

When the service was over and the last "amen" was said. I pushed past hugs and damp eyes to the back edge of the crowd. There in the distance at the far side of the cemetery near the oldest graves I found the dead tree. Beneath the tree was a dark man in a dark suit and dark glasses next to a black Mercedes. This had something to do with the agents; I just knew it. Part of me was apprehensive, but mostly, I was eager. I turned to look at my dad then I set off toward the stranger.

As I drew near, the man walked out to meet me.

"Robert Bright?" he asked again.

"I'm Robert Bright," I said.

He extended his hand, and I shook it.

"My name is Jake Massey," he said as he removed his sunglasses. "You saved my life a very long time ago."

I stared at him, then looked over my shoulder, then stared at him again.

"Jake?" I stammered. "Jacob?" I stared at him some more. He was far from the cowed, broken man who had been born into slavery. "But you're so...different," I blurted out.

He gave a genuinely warm laugh and said, "I've had a few years to improve myself." He reached inside the interior pocket of his tailored suit coat and pulled out the medallion to show me. "After all these years, I had no idea I'd see you again. When I found out you were here, I wasn't sure if you would know me. I was reluctant to introduce myself until I knew you had gone back to the time of our first meeting. I certainly didn't want to do anything to interfere with that."

"How did you find me?" I asked.

"Let's take a walk," he said.

CHAPTER 33

As we strolled along the narrow, paved walking path that went around the cemetery, the Mercedes sedan crept along with us on the outer circle drive. I tried to get a look into the car, but the windows were too darkly tinted.

"You have a driver now?" I asked Jacob.

"Yes," he said.

"I'm sorry I wasn't able to come back like I promised," I said. "But I'm glad I was able to change the outcome."

He shook his head. "Nothing changed. The Hanes family died that night just like they were supposed to. I was arrested a few days later after their bodies were discovered, because witnesses had seen me in my bloody clothes on the road near their farm. Before I could get a trial, the jailer let the night riders have me. Men in hoods took me from my jail cell, beat me, and shot me. They presumed I was dead, tied my body behind a horse, and dragged me through the town before dumping me in a garbage pit."

"Oh," I said softly. "I'm sorry."

"I had your medallion wrapped in a piece of cloth in my britches pocket the whole time. I was trying to keep it safe for you in case you returned. It's a wonder they didn't search me and steal it. I suppose they figured a man like me would have nothing of value on his person. Thankfully, when the device began the process of healing me, the cloth prevented them from seeing the blue light."

"What did they do when you went back?" I asked.

"I didn't go back. I couldn't go back," he said. "I knew I would have to leave town for good. I tried to go home, but my family thought I was a ghost or evil spirit come to haunt them. They wouldn't have anything to do with me. I couldn't make them believe otherwise, and I couldn't convince them to leave with me. I saw you hide that bag of gold near the road and —"

"You saw me? I thought I was being careful."

"Yeah, I saw. I went back for it after several days when it became evident you were not going to return for it. Anyway, I had that gold, plus the money you paid me to dispose of that dead man, plus the money and other items I had taken from the dead man's pockets. He had ten dollars in gold, a pocket watch, and the piece of white crystal. I kept fifty dollars and the watch for myself, and I left the rest on the doorstep of my little shack for my wife and kids. Then I got out of town."

"That piece of crystal you found in his pocket was why I was there," I said.

"I know that now," he replied. "But back then, I just thought it was something my wife could sell to support the kids. I'm sure it is long gone now."

Then I remembered the phone conversation I had with my dad about the bucket of rocks.

"I think the widow of one of your descendants came by the museum for an appraisal last year," I said. "They still had the crystal." Jacob was surprised and grinned. "In fact," I continued, "if they had not brought it in, I would have never gone to eighteen seventy-seven. You and I would have never met."

"In which case, I might have never found the crystal," he added.

We were both quiet for a moment contemplating the implications of that.

"Kind of blows your mind, doesn't it?" I said.

"Interesting, and where is the crystal now?"

"Gone," I said. I wasn't sure how much I should say about Thaddeus and Maribeth, so I didn't say anything. I changed the subject. "Did you know you still had family in Kinsville?"

"I knew." He nodded. "I have tried to keep tabs on them. Of course, they wouldn't know me. Everyone who knew me is long gone. I have had other families in other places. I have outlived three wives, a dozen kids, grandkids, great-grandkids—it's been tough to watch my babies grow and die of old age while I barely age at all. I would always have to leave them before they noticed my continued youth, so I'm sure they all wound up hating me. I found it best to stop doing it to myself. I have managed to avoid serious relationships for the past fifty years; it just hurts too much. Even so, I could never bring myself to get rid of the medallion. I took it off a few times, thinking I'd go ahead and grow old—once I even left it off for two whole years—but I always went back to it."

"I guess I never thought about that aspect of living a long life," I said. "It must be lonely."

"It can be, but I have my work."

I looked back at the luxury car following us. "Yeah, you've done well for yourself."

"The Nepheel are generous to their employees," he said.

I stopped. He stopped. The Mercedes stopped.

"You work for the Nepheel?" I asked.

He turned and motioned for his driver to stay there. Then he put his hand on my shoulder, and we started walking again.

"In nineteen thirty-nine, I lived in Harlem. My life was going well considering the times and the color of my skin. I had a couple of college degrees, a beautiful young wife, and a good job as a clerk in a small law office. I was in this little restaurant having coffee, and a man rushed into the joint—a white man—

191

and he was frantic and bleeding. He collapsed there in the floor, and I went to help him. When I opened his jacket, I saw he had a medallion just like mine. Before I could say anything about it, another man came in after him and opened up on us with a Tommy Gun. Then he cut down everyone in the place.

"Our medallions did their job, and he and I left out the back door before the police arrived. I told him about where I got my medallion, and he told me about the Ancients. Until that day, I still thought of you as an angel or maybe a visitor from another world. I asked to join up then and there."

"If you work for Östric, then you must know Maribeth," I said. "She was there that day when you and I first met."

"I have never met Maribeth, but I do know of her—she's sort of a legend—but I don't work for Östric. I work for Meoppes, Östric's sister."

"Oh," I said, surprised. "Okay."

He stopped and stared at me without expression. Then he said, "You don't know about Meoppes?"

"No," I said. "I only just learned about Östric the day I met you. This is all new to me."

He was obviously confused. "You mean you aren't an agent?"

"No," I laughed. "Why would you think that?"

"But what about the medallion? And you went to kill the gurelach. And you traveled through time."

"The medallion belonged to Emmet McCain, that dead man in the outhouse. The other stuff kind of just happened."

He rubbed his face and mumbled to himself, "There's been a mistake."

"What mistake?" I asked.

He stole a glance at the Mercedes then took my elbow to urge me forward. Our walk was brisker now. We got off the path, crossed over the road, and moved into a park.

"Meoppes and Östric are enemies," he said. "With all the gurelach activity in Kinsville, she sent people to scope it out. I was there when they reported back to her that Östric had agents working the town. She thinks you're one of Östric's people because Maribeth was seen at your home and business. Some of the other families think this too. In fact, you're a popular topic of conversation for a few of the families. They're all very intrigued the way you came out of nowhere, and how you were the one who secured the box. They think you're undercover—one of Östric's secret weapons."

I found this to be both flattering and absurd. "I'm in high school," I said. "Maribeth told me I wasn't even agent material. She said I was too soft."

"Where are the keys, Robert?" Jacob asked in a tone that made me uneasy. "It's really important."

"Maribeth took some of them," I said. "Virgil Strathmore took the rest. What's going on?"

"Meoppes ordered a hit on you."

I stopped again. "Say what now?"

"One of the other families did too. When I realized who you were, I volunteered for the job."

"Wait—are you here to kill me?"

He glanced back at the Mercedes again then came in close to me. "Take this," he whispered and tried to covertly pass me the medallion.

We were now far from anyone who could help me.

"Take it," he said. "I'm trying to protect you. It's important they think you are dead."

I took the medallion, and he stepped back away from me. Then he reached into his jacket again and came out with an astra.

"Jacob?"

"I will try to get word to Maribeth," he said. "Maybe Östric's clan will take you in since they are the cause of all this. It's a long shot; they aren't known for their compassion. Until then, this should buy you some time."

193

"Jacob, I'm nobody," I pleaded and held up my hands. I was about to cry. "Tell your boss there was a mix-up."

"I won't use full power," he said as the air distorted around the weapon. "Sorry, Robert, but this is going to hurt."

CHAPTER 34

When I awoke, it was night, and I was in the back seat of a limousine. The second movement of Beethoven's 7th Symphony played softly through the speakers. Next to me, and dressed in a tuxedo, was Thaddeus Soosen, He was clean, his goatee was trimmed, his mustache was waxed and curled, and his long hair was combed straight back. Maribeth sat directly across from us. She wore a short, black dress with pearls. They both looked like movie stars.

Maribeth took a sip of white wine from a stemmed glass and regarded me with either boredom or contempt. "He's finally coming around," she said dryly.

Thaddeus gave me a wink but didn't smile. "Back in the world," he said and patted my leg.

The lights of a city moved by outside the window, but I didn't recognize any of the buildings.

"Where are we going?" I asked. My mouth was dry.

"Östric wants to meet you," she said. "You've been the subject of speculation by the other families. They want you dead, and Östric likes that. He thinks it gives him an advantage to keep you around."

"How?" I asked.

"I'm sure I don't know," she replied with an eye roll and another sip of wine.

"Could I have a drink of water or something?" I asked. Thaddeus passed me a short can of ginger ale. I popped it open and drained it in one long swallow. He passed me another.

The limo slowed, and we entered a parking garage. The vehicle then pulled into a narrow room. It was an elevator, and we started down.

"How long have I been out?" I asked.

"I don't know," she said. "It's almost three now. Maybe fifteen hours?"

"I should call my dad and let him know I'm okay," I said. "He's probably worried."

"We can't allow that."

The elevator stopped, and the limousine pulled out into a massive underground cavern, the walls of which were carved out like Petra all around. I estimated the room to have a floor area of at least ten acres. Along the walls, high, arched doorways opened to more rooms of similar size. Scores of people moved around in there, each seemingly on important business. Some were on foot, but others rode craft that were similar to hovering jet skis. I sat up then pressed my face against the window so I could see up. I counted three stories using the carved windows in the wall as my guide, but each floor must have been at least twenty feet. Higher still was an impressive light source; everything was lit up like midday.

"This is Udaan," Maribeth said. "It is one of Östric's homes."

"It's huge," I said. "More like a small city."

"It does rival The Vatican," she said.

Our limousine parked next to a row of luxury vehicles in front of one of the doorways. A man in a suit rushed out and opened my door. I looked out but didn't move.

"This way, sir," he said.

Timidly, I climbed out. Maribeth and Thaddeus followed. The man shut the door.

"We're here to see Östric," Maribeth said and gave the man her wine glass.

"Very good, ma'am," the man replied. "He's expecting you."

Maribeth led the way. We passed a fountain carved out of a green stone in the likeness of a plesiosaur. Then she took an immediate right through a smaller doorway, and we entered a room with three marble statues that would have put Michelangelo's *David* to shame. Thaddeus waited next to one of the statues while Maribeth and I got on an elevator. There was only one button, and she pushed it. The door slid shut.

"There is something you should know," she said, turning to me. "There is a reason why the Nepheel have other people represent them out in the world. I wanted you to be aware they are different. Try not to act like an imbecile when you meet Östric for the first time."

"They're different how?" I asked.

The door slid open. Ahead of us was the most opulent, lavish, amazing room I have ever seen. It was gilded and bejeweled, plush and lush, yet not gaudy. The scent of the room was spicy and erotic. Two exquisite, dark-haired women met us and silently directed us toward another large room beyond.

Maribeth stepped out. I followed.

"Different how?" I repeated in a whisper.

I got my answer at that moment when Östric came out to meet us. My breath caught. He was enormous—a literal giant. He must have been fifteen feet tall, yet perfectly proportionate. His skin was smooth and chalky white, and his long red hair was braided. He wore a Sherwani—black with gold filigree.

"Maribeth," he said and bowed. "It is such a pleasure to see you again so soon. I hope you are not too disappointed that I called you away from your party."

197

Maribeth bowed and said, "Not at all. Blessings to the host."

"Come and rest," he said and motioned toward the room ahead of us, the floor of which was filled with red pillows. It was then that I noticed he had six fingers on each hand.

The silent women brought out a tray with wine, fruit, and bread.

We moved into the other room and all sat on the floor of pillows. The women distributed refreshments. I took a banana from the tray, but declined the rest. I continued to stare at Östric. All of the ancient stories about giants were true. They were real.

"Robert Bright," he said, "Maribeth tells me it was you who returned the Sarafa—the box of keys."

"Yes sir," I said.

"We have searched for it for millennia, so I am most grateful to you."

"Yes sir. You're welcome, sir."

"I am delighted that your activities have the other families so agitated."

He made a clucking noise with his tongue, and one of the women entered the room. He motioned to her, and she sat on his lap. She was child-like in size compared to him. He stroked her long, dark hair like a pet.

"It is unfortunate some of the keys were lost," he continued. "Virgil Strathmore was led astray by one of the other families." He silently stroked his pet then added, "I pity him."

Maribeth's eyes were fixed on her boss.

"He's older than the usual recruits, but I think he'll do," he said.

"I defer to your wisdom," was Maribeth's reply.

"Very well then," Östric said finally. "Welcome to the family, Robert Bright."

My eyes darted around to the faces in the room. I wasn't sure what had just happened.

"Sir?" I said. "Do you mean for me to be an agent?"

He nodded. "I do."

"I mean no disrespect, and it all sounds really exciting and cool, but I need some time to think about it. I need to talk it over with my dad. I still have a year of school left. Then there's college...."

"We will provide your education," Östric replied.

"Like a scholarship?" I said. I hoped that was what he meant, but deep down I knew it wasn't.

"You will accompany Thaddeus to the training facility," Maribeth said to me. "You leave within the hour."

"When can I talk to my dad?"

Östric turned to Maribeth. "This is why I prefer young orphans," he said. "Families and futures complicate things."

"I'll take care of it," Maribeth said.

Östric was satisfied with that answer. "Go then."

Maribeth stood and motioned for me to do the same. She then led me back to the elevator. Once inside, I said, "I don't want this. At least not like this."

"I don't like this any more than you—I think you are a pitiful recruit—but this will save your life, so be grateful."

"What about my dad? Is he in any danger? And what about Lacy?"

"I will pay them a visit," she said begrudgingly.

"You aren't going to hurt them are you?"

"Not if they cooperate. I will explain the situation to them. The girl knows enough to believe me. Let's hope she can convince your dad to believe me too."

"If I talked to them—"

"No, maybe one day, but not until the other families lose interest in you."

The elevator opened, and Thaddeus was still there. There was no more conversation. Maribeth returned to the limousine, but Thaddeus and I were escorted beyond it to another elevator. From there, the two of us were taken up. When the doors parted, we were on the windy rooftop of a skyscraper. Waiting for us was a black, windowless helicopter.

"Is that a flyin' machine?" Thaddeus yelled to me. There was a touch of fear in his eyes.

"It'll be okay," I said.

I hoped it was true.

ABOUT THE AUTHOR

Shane Gregory lives on several acres in a rural farming community in western Kentucky with his wife, two children, two cats, and a few chickens. His education background is in the visual arts. He enjoys painting, running, reading, writing, and growing his own food.

www.brainofshane.com

OTHER BOOKS BY SHANE GREGORY:
THE CLAYFIELD TRILOGY
from **Permuted Press**
The King of Clayfield
All That I See
Firebirds